BLOOD BATTLE

One hundred more yards and he'd be free!

He almost lost traction, slipping on a patch of gravel in the dark cavern. Soon he heard scampering sounds behind him and the gnashing of flesh-hungry jaws.

The huge creatures had heard him and started screeching. Screeching for his blood.

Pulling his weapon from his belt, Rockson spun once on his heels and fired his shotpistol on full automatic. The X-patterns of deadly explosive pellets spread out and demolished the front ranks of the red-eyed monsters. His clip spent, he grabbed for another but came up empty.

But the deadly horde kept on coming, crawling quickly over the torn and bloody bodies of their own dead to tear the Doomsday Warrior apart. . . .

#18: AMERICAN DREAM MACHINE
RYDER STACY

ZEBRA BOOKS
KENSINGTON PUBLISHING CORP.

Introduction

Enter now the world of Ted Rockson, the man known to all the world as the Doomsday Warrior. The time: circa A.D. 2096; the place: America.

It has been more than a hundred years since the devastating nuclear strike against the U.S. by the Soviet Union. The surprise attack had occurred right in the middle of peace negotiations that seemed to be going well. The U.S., though devastated, never surrendered, though most of its cities were wiped out, most of its population killed. A ragtag guerrilla force harassed the brutal Russian occupiers, and a sullen captive population in the new Russian slave-fortresses mounted constant revolt. Small underground complexes where freedom fighters hid and gathered strength became, over a hundred years, vast cities of "Free-fighters." The Free-fighters launched more and more sophisticated and massive attacks on the Sovs.

As a result of endless guerrilla warfare, the situation slowly changed. By the late twenty-first century, when this chapter in the Rockson saga begins, the regular Soviet forces had been forced to withdraw from American soil. The greatest threat to Free America now came from renegade, independent Russian forces. One such force was controlled by Colonel Killov, a fanatical KGB leader. Killov openly flouted the uneasy cease-fire arranged by Soviet premier Vassily and U.S. president Langford.

The other force opposing U.S.-Soviet peace arrangements was led by deposed U.S. puppet president Mikael Zhabnov. Killov was supposedly dead; but no one knew the whereabouts of the unpredictable, cowardly

General Zhabnov.

The world went about the business of trying to clean up the radioactive mess that World War III had caused. No one knew if their efforts would meet with success. Poisons were still filtering down to earth from the contaminated ionosphere. Vast areas of the planet were forbidden zones—radioactive wastelands. And day by day, the poisons still rained down. . . . It was not at all certain that life on earth—as it had been known—would survive. Perhaps just the mutant species would endure: hardy, rad-resistant creatures such as the Narga-beasts, the blood-seeking lizards of the forbidden zones, or the mutant humans, such as the Doomsday Warrior, who had the star-pattern on their backs, but otherwise looked much the same as nonmutant humans.

Rockson was a man endowed with a keen sixth sense, and a well-honed fighting talent. He had been born with an unstoppable desire to live, to endure, to triumph over all opposition. Rockson was a man who would rather die on his feet than live kneeling before the oppressor!

Chapter One

Ted Rockson's Ramjet flyer came out of a thick white cloud and the cottony blankness before his mismatched light and dark blue eyes was replaced by a spectacular vista: for a hundred miles ahead, a vast, red-hued desert spread out. The Doomsday Warrior checked his gauges. He was 6,000 feet up over the radioactive wasteland of south Utah, cruising along at a leisurely subsonic 500 miles per hour. His fuel consumption was optimal, his warning indicators all quiescent. He'd be at his destination in less than an hour. He hoped that wouldn't be too late!

It had taken Rockson three days to repair the old confiscated Soviet Ramjet and get it airborne—the three days from the time Rock had received Archer's message asking for help, giving a location far out in the wastelands of America's West. He hoped to hell that Archer was still alive when he got there. He wished that he could go a bit faster, but 500 was all this aircraft could handle. This old Sov flyer was a bag of loose bolts and jerry-rigged circuits. To go any faster meant she would probably fall apart.

"In any case," Rock thought, "I'll soon be there. To face what danger?" Rockson had no idea what peril his old friend turned hermit Archer was up against. The message hadn't gone into that. No, that would have been too easy!

The scenes of scarred and ruined canyons, jutting mesas, red painted desert land sparsely patched with vegetation, crawled by underneath Rockson. Now and then he saw the twisting lines in the sands below that indicated the path of a Narga-beast. The tails made those marks with their barbed tips. Rockson shuddered even to think of those creatures. He'd seen what the Narga-beasts had done to men—torn them apart, eaten out their guts, and then deposited eggs in their wasted bodies—eggs that within hours hatched into new, horrible additions to their evil ranks!

Slowly, the desert changed. Now and then there appeared a twisted yucca tree, or a clump of thornbushes. Rockson was pleased to see that. It meant that the radiation was fading, that the land was coming back, slowly but surely. Nature was reclaiming the man-ruined world. Whether nature would let the mad creatures known as human beings live in its domain once it was reclaimed, was another matter! Lately, it sure seemed that nature had it in for humankind, unleashing all sorts of megastorms, snowstorms in midsummer, earthquakes. It was as if the planet was trying to throw off its back the creature who had devastated it!

Rockson sighed and leaned back. He flicked a switch to put the flyer on autopilot, and then consulted the age-yellowed survey map on the seat next to him in the two-passenger craft. Yup, just as he had thought: there hadn't been a sign of life here on the last air-recon survey, just ten years ago. It was worth recording the difference.

Rockson turned on the automatic cameras in the jet's nose, to make an update for the boys back in Map Division in Century City. He glanced at the radar screen. No bogies. No challenge in the skies of America these days from Sov interceptor-jets. It was almost EERIE how the Sovs had finally packed up their bags and pulled out. The warfare against the Sovs had gone on for over a century; it had been a way of life for all Americans. Constant fighting had been a raison d'être for Rockson and his "Rock Team."

Chen, Archer, Detroit, McCaughlin, Scheransky—all of the Free-fighters—now had time aplenty on their hands. There was much to do, but to fighting men, it all seemed, well, DULL. That dullness was why Archer had lit out for parts unknown. The huge mountain man had said he couldn't stand being around people who weren't fighting. So Archer had packed up his rucksack and

8

disappeared into the wilderness where Rockson had found him so many years ago. There had been no messages from the bearded giant for three years. Not until just three days ago.

Rockson pulled Archer's message from his pocket and unfolded it. The message was a brief, cryptic scrawl in the handwriting of the mountain man, a message delivered via fax machine in the communications lab at C.C. It was nearly indecipherable, but it clearly said "Emergency" and "Danger." The message also gave map coordinates to a place called Bawl Corner. Rock smiled wryly. Archer wasn't much of a talker or a writer. But he was a hell of a fighter. If Archer needed help, the danger was severe.

He glanced at the chronometer. Fifty minutes flight time to go. Rockson put the note away and lay back in the cracked leatherette pilot's seat. His mind drifted to thoughts about his other friends. Detroit Green, the muscular black cannonball, his team's grenade-throwing expert, had been promoted to ambassador by President Langford. Detroit had been sent off to Russia. He'd been there for two years now, as "Special Envoy With Extraordinary Powers." Detroit could make policy and coordinate U.S. and Soviet cooperation. That cooperation specifically meant that both nations would endeavor to track down and bring to justice the renegades who were trying to rekindle the World War.

Rock had been there on that fateful day in Pattonville when President Langford, now old and confined to a wheelchair, had given Detroit Green the assignment. Thinking of that unlikely day, when the reluctant, muscular, black Free-fighter was drafted for the diplomatic assignment, Rock smiled. Detroit had tried to wriggle out of the job. He only wanted to stay in the U.S. But Langford said they needed the most intelligent man they could find for the job, and Detroit was that man. What irony, Rockson thought. Now the chief assistant to Premier Vassily of the Soviet Union was Ruwanda Rahallah, also a black man. And with Vassily in a more-or-less permanent coma, and near death, Rahallah was really in charge over there. Thus two black men practically ran the world now. And there was peace, real peace, for the first time in over a hundred years. Peace for a world that hadn't seen a cessation of conflict since the days of the Vikings!

As for the other members of Rockson's team: Mc-Caughlin, the Scots-background-Free-fighter, was still very much the clown, and still the best trail cook Rock had ever known. McCaughlin was in charge of expeditionary forces now that Rockson was away. The man was bigger than the side of a barn, and as gentle as a breeze. Rock missed McCaughlin's wry comments and "creeper-vine puddings." Boy could he go for a joke right now — and something to eat other than his ham sandwich.

The only Russian on the old "Rock Team," Scheransky, was over in the Soviet Union helping Detroit. Scheransky had been invaluable over the years. The blond defector from the "Evil Empire" had been a nervous and chubby technician when he served the Sovs, but had become an ardent and courageous Free-fighter. Freedom does a man good!

Chen, the Chinese American who had trained Rockson in the martial arts, was still teaching his deadly methods back in the Century City gym. The guy never seemed to age. The man with the pencil-thin mustache was on his fifth wife — Chen was not much for stable marriages. But he never missed a day of giving instructions to his classes.

Sometimes Rona would also be a part of the "Rock Team." The only female member of the team had been Rockson's lover since his teenage years. Now that the fighting was over, Rona Wallender was keeping herself busy. She was at this moment away on a relief mission to Argonville, which was recovering slowly following the crushing of a right-wing takeover there. Rockson had missed Rona these past months, but the gorgeous red-headed Amazon would be back — and all the more desirable for her long absence!

Then there was Kim. . . . He'd probably never see his

other girlfriend, Kim, again. The petite Kim was President Langford's blonde and blue-eyed daughter. Being Rockson's "other" girlfriend, she was often at odds with Rona. Rock tried to keep the girls apart, but fate usually defied his wishes. Until lately. Peace had changed even the girlfriend situation.

Kim was with her father in the restored White House. Washington was humming with diplomatic activity and endless festivities. Rock had heard that Kim was now the darling of the embassy set, and there were stories about all the glittering parties she ran in Washington. His few letters to Kim had gone unanswered. She was probably having too much fun to remember him. "What a beauty Kim was," Rockson thought with a sigh. He envisioned her petite yet full-breasted body, her alabaster skin, her bright blue eyes . . . and the childlike, tender love she made with him.

Rockson pulled his thoughts away from the winsome vision and looked out over the changing terrain. There was water below now—a twisting river, and a high waterfall coming off a butte. The brilliantly sunlit desert made him gasp in appreciation of its beauty. Until he saw the festering old mile-wide nuke bomb crater to the north. Its fetid mists were probably hiding all sorts of evil radgrowths. He'd been down in those hellholes more than once. Never again!

Another glance at the clock: twenty minutes until he reached his destination. And then what? The terrain was mighty rugged below. Rock sure hoped there would be a good landing spot when he got there. These old Russian jobbies took a mighty *long* time to slow down, once they landed!

Assuming he'd make a safe landing, he had no idea what kind of trouble he'd find. But Rockson figured he'd be up to most challenges, even though he was alone. After all, he had his shotpistol, capable of firing a dozen rounds of explosive shotgun pellets. He had a fully auto-fire Liberator smg, and various grenades. That equipment,

11

plus his keen fighting abilities, should do the trick against any of the usual bugaboos, such as mutant animals, tribes of crazies or cannibals, or Red renegades.

There were no more regular Sov forces in America, no more fortress city-prisons bristling with artillery, no more neo-Nazi armies under Colonel Killov. Killov was dead — drowned in a billion gallons of water from a burst dam. Or was Killov dead? The KGB leader had a habit of rising from the dead. . . . It was as if Killov had a pact with the Dark One himself. Rock didn't trust the man not to rise up again. But aside from that gruesome possibility, what the hell *was* the threat out there? What was Archer fighting against? If only Rock had been TOLD what to expect. Should he have brought along the heavy, tripod-mounted 73-mm Narga-beast gun?

The old Sov plane's left engine coughed. Rockson reached to the control panel and enriched the fuel mixture a bit. He frowned. Both engines were running hot. This bag of bolts should make it, but if it didn't, there was always the parachute. Rockson had trekked great distances before.

The left engine coughed again, and Rock's brow furrowed a bit. He fiddled with the fuel mixture. Both needles denoting engine temperature were up into the red. One hundred thirty miles to go. God, what more could he do to keep it aloft? Maybe he should fly lower, get into thicker air? That *might* help the engines. But then, if the plane went down, there wouldn't be time enough to chute to safety.

Rockson thought for a minisecond and decided to chance it. He didn't relish walking a hundred miles, and besides, Archer was in danger. Maybe seconds would matter. So Rock lowered the Sov craft until it was skimming over the rolling hills littered with boulders. He even went between two towering buttes. Altitude 200 feet! Engines getting cooler.

Sharp left! Avoid the damned pillar of stone dead ahead! Rockson deftly maneuvered the craft past the

12

danger. Flying at this altitude keeps you on your toes! No auto-guidance on this baby, you have to fly by the seat of your pants! There was a certain thrill to all of this, and Rockson felt it now. Ah, this was the way it used to be, just man and machine, working together, *without* the damned computers!

The left engine blew up. And at the same time as the pieces flew in all directions in a fiery shower, the right engine just quit of its own accord. The awesome silence — except for the wind rushing by and the flutter of a long trail of black smoke in the rear — made Rock's hair stand on end.

He was hitting the restart button but nothing was happening. He coasted her up to 400 feet. Now there were just seconds to act. Should he try to glide her in? Or should he hit the chute? No, he'd worked too long and hard to restore this baby, to make this Sov junker fly. He wouldn't let her crash! He'd try for a landing!

Luckily, there appeared to be plenty of flat land between the buttes ahead. He hit the button to dump the remaining fuel and get a few more seconds maneuvering time from lightening it up a bit. "Okay," Rockson mumbled, "let's take her in. Here goes nothing."

But as he dove, the gentle, flat land ahead became a nightmare maze of canyons and huge boulders. *Oh shit*, now what?

His mutant instincts came into play. His sixth sense *had to* be at work now, for there was no way of guessing which canyon to roar down into. Rockson's hand caressed the heavy control stick. He was sensing, feeling where to direct her.

He felt his hand jiggle the stick a bit to the left. He knew that if he took the left fork in the canyon ahead, there would be a chance! Just a small chance.

Chapter Two

His air speed was 500 knots — 470 — 420. There was nothing in the books about how to fly a jet like this as a goddamned glider! But there *was* something in his *gut* that told him what to do.

Flying by the seat of his pants, Rockson *felt* the maneuvers he should take. He veered suddenly to the left, down a narrow canyon, sensing a way to open ground. He rocked the jet around a cylindrical stone outcropping, then tore between two huge boulders. The wingtips just missed being hit.

Suddenly he was not sure where to go. He had to decide — cliff coming up, dead ahead. He guessed left, and that soon proved wrong. The wings were too wide to make it between the narrow canyon walls. *Unless —*

Rockson turned the craft sharply sideways and fit through with wings up and down, and made it out into a wider canyon. Good, but he'd lost some more altitude in that maneuver. The area ahead was littered with boulders. Where the hell is a flat area?

Now tight left, his sixth sense told him. His plane swooped low over some rolling sand dunes. His altitude was 300, 250 — air speed now 270, 230 — he knew she'd drop like a rock at 160 knots. He'd have to bring it in before then — but where?

Altitude 170. The canyon was wide here, but filled with jagged boulders. And now something new appeared — a raging river right in the middle of the scattered boulders. A torrential rapids that would shame the Colorado River's meek white foams! Come on, flat ground, come on . . .

Altitude 100 feet, speed 165.

This was it. Stubby pine trees flashed below his wings now. It had been all desolation before, and now, all of a sudden, these pine trees. The damned trees were worse than the big rocks. He was going to hit them.

Wait. Over there. Some reddish flatlands ahead, the pines fading out. Rockson's craft just cleared the last pine trees, skimming off the topmost branches. There was a small clearing ahead, alongside the raging river. The river, Rockson saw, emerged from a waterfall in a mist-shrouded cliff *dead ahead*. The smooth cliff rose thousands of feet high. No way over THAT baby! Speed 160—GOTTA TAKE HER IN!

Another huge boulder right ahead, with a scruffy pine on it!

Can't clear it! Rockson jerked in his seat as the belly of his craft scraped the obstacle. Pieces of rock and pine needles and sticky pine cones were jammed onto the wing tips. Altitude 70, 60, 30. Clear sand ahead. For a second he clutched the lever for the landing gear, then desisted. A belly landing was better on soft sand. Otherwise, the wheels would jam, and the plane would tumble over the minute he hit.

Rockson lifted the plane's nose at the last second, then shielded his face with his arms.

He hit the ground hard, but the plane didn't break up, at least not right away. He was skidding on the metal belly. Sparks and then flames erupted all around him as he jerked violently against the restrainer straps. He watched wide-eyed as the wings were shorn off by jutting rocks. That slowed his mangled cockpit compartment some more, but still the plane—what was left of it—slid forward toward the high wall of rock at the end of the canyon. Rockson was barreling toward a looming wall of pink granite death. He expected to be smashed like a bug in a second.

The sickening screech of metal and the flames were everywhere around him now; his chances of dying from being smashed were pitted against being burned alive. He bet he would hit the wall first.

The wall of the canyon was coming up fast, maybe 150 miles per hour. He'd win the bet.

What the hell? He saw, strung across the canyon before him, a series of clothesline-thick white ropes. The torn-up plane hit them hard, tore through the first two or three ropes. But the ropes slowed its fatal hurtle toward oblivion. The next two or three lateral ropes grabbed at the plane's bent nose and didn't let go. Ten feet from the vertical wall of rock, and his certain death, the plane stopped with a gutwrenching jerk.

The control panel burst into flames and now the billowing, black, plastic-fed smoke threatened to choke the pilot. Rock tore at his restraining straps. They wouldn't come loose!

"Have to cut them off!" he shouted to no one in particular. Good idea but hell, no knife! Rockson steeled his muscles and jerked himself upward two or three times, his body driven by a bolt of adrenaline that could have revived a thousand heart patients. He tore the straps apart and leaped from the seat, trailing the remnants of the nylon safety straps. "Have to get out. Now!" he screamed at himself.

So Rockson rushed through the cramped and crumpled cabin and spun the door's circular lock: no go. It was bent in, the frame wouldn't let go! Thick, plastic-fueled smoke now curled about his body. The door simply had to give.

Rockson stepped back and, holding onto the twisted girders on both sides of him, delivered the most powerful double drop-kick of his entire career.

The bent door flew out and away. Fire and smoke and white hot sparks poured onto him. Rock jumped out through the billowing wall of fire before him. He hit the gravel and rolled through sharp, hot metal debris, wincing in pain as the debris cut through his fire-resistant flight suit and into his skin. Once he hit the

16

ground he kept rolling over and over until his body was out onto cool brown sand. Then he beat out the flames that had begun to consume his sleeves and the sock-tops sticking out of his combat boots.

After that was taken care of, Rockson crawled like a motherfucker away from the heat. No time to even stand up, he had to get away from the jet as fast as he could. There were explosive things in that plane: the heavy caliber ammo left in the nose cannon might go off any second—and the grenades.

KABOOM! The force of the explosion threw him twenty feet.

After the orange ball of flame rose overhead, Rockson dug his face out of the sand and sat up. He watched the mushroom-shaped cloud rising in the canyon. So much for the Soviet plane—and all those hours of work patching it. Obviously he had missed fixing something! Rockson wondered what it was. He grimaced as he stood and surveyed the wreckage of his sky-machine. Not much left. He nonchalantly picked a piece of sharp metal out of his forearm, tossed it away, and started walking away from all the damage; his mind not dwelling on his luck but on all that fucking work repairing the old jet down the drain! Only after a while did he mutter, "Hell, who cares, I'm alive!"

When he took his first step, his ankles hurt. Sprained ankle? Better not be. As he pranced around on them, they hurt less and less. Thank heaven for that!

Next business: Where was he? The map! Was the fucking map in the plane?

He fumbled around in his flight suit, and felt a slight rectangular bulge. "Ah, there it is, right in my pocket." Rockson pulled out the map, opened it, and in the fading light studied it carefully. After a while he decided that he was in a place the map called Spider Canyon, about thirty-seven miles short of his intended destination. A long walk, but nowhere near impossible. Spider Canyon was a long, many-branched canyon

17

located in a plateau that was a mile high. At this height, in this part of America, the night would be hell-cold. Arctic cold. And he had no parka. *That* had burned up in the jet.

Might as well start walking—which way? Northeast. Climb up that granite face before dark, get his bearings with the stars. Sky is clear, Rockson reassured himself, the stars should be bright tonight. He could find the way.

Inventory of supplies: Matches for a fire, a map. Brains and brawn. Things could be worse. How about weapons? *Oh God!*

Rock ran back to the fragmented smoking wreckage and dug around through the scorched debris. He was relieved when finally his hands uncovered his shotpistol. It was looking bad, but it was still functional. He found some ammo in a steel case. Not much—100 rounds. The Liberator rifle was a fused mess. He lifted its melted mass, then threw it down in disgust.

He looked up at the sky above him. The stars were already coming out, along with flickers of blue-green aurora. A cold wind arose. With the shotpistol recovered, things weren't really so bad. Should he really climb *now?* As cold as it was here in the canyon, it would be much colder up on the plateau. There would be driftwood to make a fire, near the river. And water—maybe a fish dinner.

Rock quickly decided to stay the night in the canyon. He'd stay warm with a cozy fire, sheltered from the winds by the canyon walls. He'd get going bright and early in the morning. Archer needed him alive, after all.

He headed down toward the river, back along the skid marks and gouges from the crash landing. It was not long before Rockson saw the ripped white lines on the dirt—the mysterious ropes that had saved his life by slowing the plane. Funny, he had almost forgotten about them. He went over to the first rope, lying torn

18

and twisted. He bent down and found that it was warm and sticky to the touch. Maybe it was some sort of creep-vine. He pulled his hand away with some difficulty. Shit, if it was a creeper, it could be dangerous. Creepers can tangle you in two seconds. He shouldn't be touching one.

He noticed other broken "ropes" scattered about. They didn't move, yet he kept his fingers on the butt of the shotpistol he had jammed into his waistband. He'd tangled with all sorts of crawl-vines before. The mutant arms of such plants could wind about your ankles and drag you into the throat of a carnivorous plant in a flash! One of the nifty threats created in the hundred years of radiation since the war.

Rockson edged away from the "ropes," though they continued to remain inert. He took a more circuitous path toward the raging rapids. He could hear the turgid water's song of violence. He spotted some driftwood on the shore. When Rockson went toward the twisted branches, he came across animal tracks. Not those of hooves, like a deer's. The prints were made by three-toed paws.

Very peculiar tracks. He bent down and studied them carefully. A strange, pungent odor came into his nostrils, of something like musk. The tracks were too numerous, too closely packed, for one thing. Maybe the animals that had made them were in a tightly packed bunch.

Rockson followed them along. The tracks were fresher and fresher as he walked toward the river. Mountain lions? By the shallowness depth of the prints, the creatures weren't very big, he decided. Maybe three feet high. Well, he could handle *that* kind of cat. Rockson was powerfully thirsty now, and the water ahead was greatly inviting. Rockson walked on in a hurry — and then paused in mid-stride. What if the creatures that had made the tracks *weren't* animals? What if they were insects? Many-legged insects could have made

19

those tracks. His heart froze as if an icicle had struck it. If the creatures were insects they were pretty large.

Spider Canyon. Shit. This place was *called* Spider Canyon. Now the mysterious ropes that had slowed his crash landing made sense. They weren't ropes! They weren't creeper vines! They were spider webs!

Just then he heard scuttling noises and dropped quickly to the ground. The noises ceased. After a long while of utter silence Rockson crawled stealthily up to the top of a low knoll and peered toward the river. There, in the dim twilight, he saw a dozen three-foot-wide, furry white spiders! The monster arachnids were devouring the carcass of an antelope-type creature. The carcass was caught up in some of those very same white "ropes" that had saved his life. More spiders came and went.

The hairy white spiders evidently hung around the water line, inside those piles of driftwood. Dens for spiders! They waited for thirsty animals or for humans such as Rockson. The poor animal they had in their clutches now had probably been seeking a little drink. Now it was being torn apart and devoured. The spiders' rip-jaws made unpleasant slurping sounds.

Rock had seen and heard enough. He'd stay thirsty tonight! He probably could devastate that pack of spiders with the shotpistol, but there were other packs of the bastards around. His ass was grass if he stayed around here!

He crawled slowly, silently, back down the way he'd come, and scanned the canyon walls: vertical, with few handholds, if any. And it was getting dark. But those feeding sounds made him decide. Handholds or no handholds, he'd try a climb. That was better than becoming a meal for the chittering arachnid gourmets behind him. He assumed they were the kind of heavy, land-roving spiders that *didn't* climb walls. A shaky assumption, but one that gave him *some* comfort! He crouch-ran toward the rock escarpment, holding his shotpistol in his right hand. The flickering aurora above seemed shaped like a skeletal hand. In the near darkness, Rockson almost ran into another set of the sticky horizontal spider-ropes. These were fresher than the ones that had snagged his airplane. If Rockson had fallen onto them . . . well, he would have been stuck there until visitors came — white furry visitors.

He slowly circled the web-rope network, not seeing any net manager around. He again ran. This time he ran flat out. The roar of the water should cover his footfalls — he hoped. Jesse Owens would have been left in his dust!

Rockson's night vision was excellent, and as he raced along, he studied the sheer rock face dead ahead for danger. There were no web-ropes that he could *see* on the cliff, and no place for the spider-things to hide.

One hundred more yards! He'd better get there while that pack of carnivorous spiders was still busy. He almost lost traction, slipping on a patch of strewn gravel. That made noise, and soon he heard scampering sounds behind him, and the sounds of slavering jaws. It quickly sounded like a horde of little schnauzer dogs were right on his heels.

The spiders started screeching for blood — his blood. One quick look back. They were gaining!

They were going to get to him at the same time he got to the cliff! Pulling his weapon from his belt, Rockson spun once on his heels and fired his shotpistol on full automatic. The X-patterns of deadly explosive pellets spread out and demolished the foremost ranks of the red-eyed bastards. In a second he'd used up a whole clip.

More of the things just came rushing over the torn and bloody bodies.

This wasn't going to work!

21

Chapter Three

The furry white eight-legged creatures snapped their sharp, drippy mandibles right at Rockson's boots, but by then he was up on the cliff, his fingers and feet searching out and finding the tiny indentations in the rock, just in time. In a second, as the spiders, snarling in rage, tried to jump up on his back, Rockson was already twenty feet up the wall, climbing with all his mutant survival-instincts on full go. Imperceptible hand- and-boot holds, tiny irregularities that no normal human climber could have managed to secure himself on, were as good as a staircase to the desperate Doomsday Warrior. Nothing seemed less desirable at the moment to Rockson than falling, winding up as the evening meal of the drooling bunch of eight-legged bastards screeching and yapping below him.

For a second Rock worried that they might be able to climb walls, but as he got further and further up, the carnivore-spiders continued merely to jump up and fall back. The cliff surface became more irregular after a time, with lots of easy grips. This cliff, Rockson realized, was ready made for climbing. Still, it was pretty dark now, and he told himself not to grow too confident. There were a good 2,000 feet left to climb.

Rockson, the immediate danger behind him, began pacing his climb, taking it easy, despite the disgusting slavering of the spiders. When he looked back down to see how far he'd come in twenty minutes, he was disgusted and repelled to see the whole canyon below covered with spiders, *millions* of them. They seemed to reflect the faint starlight, almost to glow. "Must be a shortage of meat in the area! Or maybe they particularly like two-legged suppers! Is it my Desperado cologne?"

22

Worst of all, the spiders were climbing over one another. It was like rush hour in Manhattan down there. They just kept coming. God, if he only had a grenade! The damned things were piling up ten, twenty, thirty deep, crushing one another to get to Rockson! *No more taking it easy!*

Rockson climbed as fast as he could now, and that was plenty fast! After about another thousand feet of breathtaking ascent he chanced again looking back down. And with relief he noted that the piles of spiders hadn't increased much in height. Rockson listened, but didn't hear anything except the raging river. It looked eerily alive from up this far. The foaming, turgid waters were luminescent in the light of the rising moon.

Rockson, though evidently out of range of the creatures, didn't slacken his pace. His fingertips were raw and strained, his toes felt like raw tortured meat inside his supple leather boots. There were just another hundred feet or so to reach the top. He did the distance in about twenty seconds.

When his fingers crawled over the edge, they touched sand. He got one elbow, then the next up over the edge and crawled onto the gritty surface. He lay flat on his aching back, utterly exhausted. Rockson stared up at the brilliant crescent moon and the fields of crystal stars. The red star Regulus was high up in the west, which, at this time of year, made it about midnight. A glance at the Big Dipper, which cruised upside down in the north, confirmed the time-guess.

Within minutes Rockson's remarkable mutant ability to recover from exertion worked its wonders. His breaths came in more regular and less sharp intakes, and he began to feel the bitter cold. Though he wanted to stand up and get moving, to try to get warm, he did not move. He just listened. For there could be spiders or—other things—up here, too. He watched random meteors from time to time flit cross the strewn-diamond starfields. Now and then a pulse of deadly radioactive energy—the left-

23

overs of a war that had happened over a hundred years ago — briefly created a smoky, twisting, purple curtain in the ionosphere. When he was quite sure nothing lurked nearby, Rock decided he HAD TO move. He was freezing.

The minute he tried to get up, he started to hurt. Every muscle in his body had, evidently, been strained to the utmost by his mad climb to safety. Rockson took a deep breath and stood up anyway, countering the pain with his willpower, which was immense. His ankles throbbed, his leg tendons felt like rusted bridge cables. But he could walk, that was the important thing. As for the pain . . . maybe something could be done about it.

He searched in his beltpack for the antiswelling pills and found the little blue tablets. He palmed two of them, brought them up to his mouth, and swallowed them with a gulp. He barely got them down. After all, he was bone dry.

"Have to get water." His voice sounded cracked and parched. He jumped up and down, trying to keep numbness away. As the pains in his limbs eased, Rockson, sighting up the stars, turned and headed northeast.

After an hour of steady plodding on flat surface, he came upon a spectacular rock formation. Glowing in the low moon's yellow light was a sand- and wind-carved arch of stone. It was about a hundred feet high and twice as wide. This, he thought, had to be the so-called Utah Rainbow, clearly delineated upon his map. The moon was bright enough for his mismatched blue mutant-eyes to verify that fact.

Rockson smiled wryly. He was only twenty-three miles from his intended destination. Better than he had hoped when he crash-landed. But even twenty-three miles could be a deadly distance if he didn't get some water soon; it might as well be a hundred. And the cold was worse than he'd expected. Must be minus fifty already. And the night was young! If he was numb with the cold now, what about in an hour? He surveyed the moonlit irregular rocks near

24

the arch and considered crawling into a crevasse in the sandstone formations, to try to rest and keep warm till dawn.

No, he'd die here for sure if he did that! "Keep walking," he mumbled to himself. "Walk until you find something to set fire to with the matches." He had to look for some dry grass to gather, or twigs. He had to use his eyes, look for live vegetation — for live vegetation might mean water.

He was staggering after just an hour. But Rock kept his head high, trying to tough it out, ignore the cold. He kept telling himself that he could walk till dawn if necessary. Yeah, believe it!

As the first rosy fingers of dawn wriggled out of the grave of a bitter cold corpse of earth, Rockson's numb and frozen eyes beheld a clump of twisted, dried-out pine trees dead ahead. He rushed over to them, half stumbling over his own numbed feet, and fell upon the scattered brown needles. Madly he gathered together a pile of the dry stuff, and with shaking bluish hands added a few twigs to the pile. Then Rockson took out his matches and struck one. It lit cheerily. He ignited the kindling to start a campfire. He kneeled by it, keeping it from the constant west wind, and absorbed its growing warmth until he almost burned his pants off. He found some larger branches and added them to the flames.

By the time the sun peeked red over the horizon, Rockson was on his way to getting warm. And that meant he had another thing in mind now: water! "Got to have water!" His wild eyes searched around like radar beacons, and soon alighted on some squat, round cacti, a whole mess of them, each about a foot wide. Cacti! Most postnuke cacti were poisonous. And yet . . . these looked very green and fresh, beckoning in the sunlight.

"Barrel-babies!" Rockson gasped out loud the popular name of the little cactus that Century City citizens had

25

learned over the years contained small quantities of bitter but drinkable sap. He fairly leapt for the plants. He tore open with his belt-knife the first one he reached and sucked up every ounce of the moisture in its pulpy center. Sure was bitter! But what the hell. It was wet!

After he indulged himself on six other barrel-babies, he'd had enough. Rockson half walked, half crawled back to the now-substantial campfire and threw a few more larger sticks upon it. He was still cold, so he half curled around the flames. A feather bed in Century City's honeymoon suites never felt as soft as the hard ground below his bones at that moment. Rockson kept his shotpistol in his right hand as he closed his eyes and fell asleep.

When he awoke he knew he had slept for hours. The sun was halfway up in the velvet purple sky. Some ravenlike birds were squawking and twittering in the dead pines nearby. Perhaps they were serenading him. Congratulating a survivor. The birds soon tired of his attempts to mimic their cries, and flew over and pecked at the remains of the cacti that he had torn apart. They seemed as thirsty as he had been, pecking at the pulp with gusto. Rockson smiled and sat up and yawned. He looked around and, feeling the weight of his gun in his right hand, stuck the shotpistol back in his waistband.

Rockson made for a dead pine tree and relieved his bladder — what little there was to relieve — on the gnarled bark. He rubbed his hands together, stomped his feet. They were still a little numb. After all, it *was* winter. But the temperature was rising by the second. Perhaps it would make it all the way into the twenties today, if the clouds didn't cover the sun. A regular tropical resort!

He scratched at his face and rubbed his eyes and then headed northeast again, as best he could figure the direction. Before he did so, however, he gathered up some of the smaller barrel-babies scattered in the sands. He needed a way to carry them, but that was no problem. He tied some pine twigs together to form a sort of rough basket, and put the water-cacti inside it.

He whistled as he set off. What more could a twenty-first century man ask? He had a blue sky to walk under, some water in his gut, and a happy song to whistle.

Soon he stopped whistling. And he walked. And walked. In a few hours, he realized the temperature was defying his earlier guestimate. It was hotter than hell. Maybe 110 degrees! Rockson had quickly used up all the little cacti he'd carried along, and so he threw away the basket. He walked on. Crazy weather. Crazy world . . .

Six more hours of walking and it was near sunset. His once-cheery thoughts were now drifting to melancholy subjects. He was hungry. And maybe lost. Everything looked pretty much the same out here. And most of all he was stupid: he should have saved the basket for making a fire! How many miles back had he left it? Too far. There was nothing but barren waste all around.

He sat down on a flat rock, sighed, and took out the map again. He looked all around him at the fields of boulders, the rolling dry terrain. He was in a blank part of the map now. Best he could figure, he should be near the location from which Archer had sent his distress signal. At least he hoped so. But without landmarks, without a compass or a sextant . . . Hell, Archer's mysterious Bawl Corner could be right over the rise to the left — or to the right. Or straight ahead. Or behind him. He could have overshot it, off course by a mere mile or so.

Rockson, his mind cloudy with exhaustion, and with a foul mood descending on him, nevertheless did the bright thing. He decided to walk up the steepest incline and survey the area from there. No sense just walking at random. Gain some altitude, take a look-see before it was dark again.

When he started up the dusty rise to the left he found something he didn't much like: tracks. The tracks of several pawed creatures. Big-pawed mothers.

Oh shit, what was this now? Some huge wolves to

contend with? Some Narga-beasts? He put his hand on the reassuring butt of his shotpistol. Comforted by its presence, he continued to the top of the hill.

The tracks converged with other, similar tracks at the top, then headed off to the west. He realized that they had been made when the ground was muddy. They must be days, weeks old, he told himself. Hell, the creatures that made those tracks could have been prehistoric! Well, at least a *week* prehistoric. Shielding his eyes from the setting sun, he didn't see anything like a settlement in any direction. But he wasn't up very high. All around Rockson were massive boulders, each higher than a man. Rockson figured out a way to clamber from one to the other, to get on top of the highest one. He began to do so. But as he jumped up on the first boulder, he felt a sudden strange apprehension.

Something was near.

Had he heard it, or smelled it? Or had he just sensed it with his mutant instincts? No matter. If there was something — or someone — nearby . . . Get the shotpistol out.

As he reached for the weapon, he froze, crouching. Rock's muscles tensed, his dry lips opened to breath in extra gulps of the hot air. He was ready. He stood there in a crouch, slowly turning, surveying every concealment area, his shotpistol cocked in his hand, his finger on the trigger.

He did a full circle. Nothing. Maybe he was going nuts.

He waited for a time, and then climbed to the highest boulder, well aware that he was now a perfect target for a sniper. But the feeling of danger had passed. Perhaps something or someone had passed near him, passed by without seeing him. He shuddered, imagining all sorts of toothy monsters.

He had a good view here. On all the horizons north, south, east, and west were nothing but more boulders and sand and scrub pines. Rockson climbed down from his lofty place, went down the rubbled slope, heading northeast — he hoped — once more.

With just the setting sun's position to guide him, Rock couldn't be absolutely sure of direction. But hell, what IS sure in life? Except death. That is sure.

Eventually he came to another rise, this one composed of reddish soil and, blessedly, clogged with blueberry bushes. He ate his fill of the juicy godsends, slobbering them down like a mad bear. Sated, Rockson climbed to the bald top of the blueberry hill, and in the twilight he saw it: a settlement. To his amazement, Rockson was staring down into a verdant valley. There were twentieth century ruins down there — the leftover cracked pavement of an old road, and some large concrete-block buildings. Each building was surrounded by grass-pocked parking lots. But what attracted his attentions most was the sole sign of life down there. From the largest building, which looked like an airplane hangar, curled some black smoke. The smoke was coming from a huge shiny new metal chimney pipe. The pipe looked like it had been jerry-rigged very poorly — and very recently. It wouldn't stand much of a wind, that was for damn sure.

An ancient, huge advertising sign hung half-collapsed at the edge of the structure's old parking lot entrance. The rusty words said BOWL G C N ER. Probably once had said BOWLING CENTER.

Yes. Rock smiled. This must be the Bawl Corner of Archer's message! The gentle giant he had come so far to rescue *could* be the one making all the smoke. After all, Archer was never very good at making clean-burning campfires! "Maybe the danger has passed. Maybe we could have a drink together, laugh about the long trip I've taken for no reason. . . ."

"Then again," Rockson cautioned himself, "it could be some enemy down there making that smoke. Maybe some cannibals are cooking up Archer's massive fatty body! Grim thought! But could be right! Better go down cautiously."

Rockson scrambled down the steep, weed-strewn incline onto the flat surface of the old parking lot. He took cover behind the disintegrating hulk of an old oil truck. You could still see EXXON in red on its side. The truck cannister must have been made of aluminum.

Something caught his foot in the near total dark. A foul, musty smell of death assailed his nostrils, almost making him gag. Rock had found the first of many bodies he was to discover moldering away in that asphalt charnel ground!

His vision was very keen, so he could see in the starlight that the deceased were all men, all in unmarked gray uniforms. They were mean-looking mothers, each and every one. The bodies all had had their guts blown out of their stomachs. Some of the bodies were crawling with large ants and grasshoppers, insects that seemed not to know it was winter and that they shouldn't be out walking around now. Rockson drew the obvious conclusions.

No doubt about it, there were all the signs of a recent battle here. There were bullet holes in the rusted cars and trucks, and craters made by some sort of artillery fire in the parking lot's weeded surface. And there was one big hole in the wall of the large building as well. Right in the middle of the bowling center itself. A mortar had made that hole.

Rockson ducked from cover to cover, coming closer and closer to the building. He was heading as silently as he could manage for the man-sized shell hole in the wall.

He was just ten feet from that hole, hidden behind the carcass of a twentieth century RV, when a cold thing touched his left temple. It felt like a gun barrel. No, make that a double gun barrel. The wide double aperture of a twin 10-gauge shotgun was pressed hard against his head.

Chapter Four

Rockson was most definitely slipping! No one had been able to sneak up on Rockson like that in a long, long time. Having no other alternative, Rockson froze in place, not moving a hair. He half winced, expecting the shot that would send his brains flying in a hundred directions. But that didn't happen. As he took a few short breaths he inhaled body odor. That would be the person with the shotgun. The gunner smelled like a wet bear! As a matter of fact, he *stank* to high heaven.

A gruff, gravelly voice snarled out, "STAY still!"

"I'm not going anywhere," Rock replied. That voice sounded MIGHTY familiar. And that smell, come to think of it. Rock moved his head a tiny bit, so that he could put the corner of his vision over to the side. He saw the mountainous man holding the weapon. The huge man was wearing a wide-brimmed leather hat, and was covered in furs crudely sewn together. He had a huge, tangled black beard, with red and white strands in it. The beard was stuck with old pieces of chewing tobacco and what must have been pieces of food—the menu of a month. The dark, beady eyes were calm and direct, if a bit blank. He *knew* this fellow.

Rockson said, in a soft voice, "Archer, it's me Archer! You fuckhead, put down that shotgun!"

The shotgun didn't move. "Huh? Rockson?"

"Yes, you heard me. It's your old pal, the Doomsday Warrior, come to rescue you. Is this anyway to treat—"

Now the barrels of the shotgun lifted away from his temple. Rockson turned slowly and put his steady, ice-chip blue eyes upon the mountain man's big brown orbs. "Yeah, it's *me!*," he complained. "Why, you stupid bastard!

31

You coulda killed me!"

The man, still holding the shotgun in one meaty hand, threw out his arms to give Rock a big bear hug. A wide, candy-eating grin broadened on the lips above the tangled beard. "Rock! You came!"

As Archer nearly squeezed the life out of his would-be rescuer, both barrels of the shotgun discharged. They blasted a hole a foot deep in the soil right next to their feet. Rock's ears rang, and he could hardly hear for the next few seconds. He checked to see that his feet were still on his body — they were.

Archer looked embarrassed. "Sorry! Hair trigger!" He stepped back, red-faced, looking like a child about to be admonished for wetting his pants.

Rock just frowned. "Okay Arch, what's the big emergency? Tell me why I came here."

"See bodies? It over now!" the big man replied. He smiled broadly once more. "Big bad gang. But I MORE bad!" Archer punched Rock on the shoulder in a friendly gesture and nearly knocked the Doomsday Warrior down. "Come!"

"I will, if you stop shouting!"

"OK," Archer said more softly. "Sorry. I make up little mistake with gun! You come! Eat! Drink! Later screw nice girl! Me happy. You no forget Archer! Come we have beers!"

Rock nodded and trudged along beside the huge man, who headed, not for the hole in the building, but for a door further down along the same wall. Rock was still miffed about the near accident to his braincase, and demanded more explanation for the urgent message, as they walked. He received a terse elaboration of the events that had forced Archer to send the message: a gang of marauders called the Black Magic Boys had surrounded Archer's little retirement place and given him a hard time for a week. It had been Archer against about twenty well-armed men. Archer had been besieged and desperate when he sent the message. Then he'd had a neat idea. He let them break in where he stored his liquor supply: a thousand cartons of twentieth century Scotch. Then, as the gangsters became too drunk to fight, Archer sneaked around, taking them out one by one, with this very same hair-trigger blunderbuss.

"Well, I'm glad that you survived," Rock muttered as Archer held the door open, "but next time send a nevermind message, OK?"

"You no come see me, if I not in danger?" Archer looked hurt. "You no miss me?"

"It's not that, pal," Rock replied, feeling guilty. He had hurt the big man's feelings. Archer was like a kid. "It's just that I wouldn't have hurried here. I would have spent a little more time fixing up the junk heap that I crash-landed forty miles back!"

"You hurt?" Archer looked pained. "I see burn marks, torn clothes. . . . You hurt?" He was leading Rock through a warehouse-sized room half-filled with crates marked AMF.

"No, I'm OK, Arch. No problem landing at all," Rock lied. "And it was an easy walk to get here. Just a few spiders tried to bite me along the way, just a little thirsty, that's all."

Archer slapped him on the back again. "Good! I glad no problem!" They entered a small room, one with some stuffed, paisley-print furniture and a big Ben Franklin coal stove in it. The stove was almost red hot. The big round pipe leading up from the stove into the ceiling was, no doubt, the source of the smoke Rock had seen from the hill. The Vatican made less smoke choosing a pope!

There were no windows, but still there was lots of light in the room, cast from several brightly burning Coleman lamps placed on tables around the place. The room smelled like spilled draft beer.

"Home!" Archer exclaimed. "Is Nice!" He yelled this, forgetting Rock's admonishment about not shouting.

Rockson wasn't so sure. The place Archer called home was a virtual pigsty. Its floors and table surfaces, and its sofa and chairs, were littered with the remains of many

33

well-chewed, poorly cooked chickens. There were crumbling tabloid newspapers scattered everywhere, papers with names such as *National Enquirer* and *Weekly World News*. They dated from the late twentieth century, and had headlines that said "I WAS RAPED BY SPACE ALIENS (and have the baby to prove it)" or "WOMAN LIVED SEVEN YEARS TRAPPED IN ABANDONED GAS STATION REST ROOM." Rockson picked one crumbling tabloid up and asked, "Arch, you read these things?"

"Yes. Very good stories!"

"Hmmm." Rock set the tabloid down. He wiped a finger over the dust on a little end table full of chicken bones and frowned. Archer caught Rock's expression and said, "This not best part of place, pal. Come see!" The big man opened a second door and they went on into a vast chamber dimly lit by skylights high above. It was cold in there.

"Well, I'll be!" Rock exclaimed. They were in an ancient bowling alley. There were two dozen wooden-floored lanes. And AMF pin spotters—some with dusty pins still standing in them—waiting for a strike for over a hundred years, There were lines of bowling balls, too. Rock smiled and went over to one line of big black balls and was about to stuff two fingers into the little holes in one ball to pick it up and throw it. But just then a mean-looking caterpillar, a red one full of spikes, crawled out of one of the fingerholds. Rock decided to forgo the experience! He'd stick to snooker.

He noted now that half the lanes had their flooring ripped up. That explained the wood and varnish smell coming from the old stove back in Archer's pigsty room. The giant was gradually consuming his own domicile to keep warm. There must be years worth of flooring left to burn. "Nice," Rockson said, not knowing what he was supposed to say. "Very nice place."

Archer's chest swelled and he led Rock back into the warmer small room. "Sit, Drink!" Archer demanded, opening a cabinet and handing Rockson an ancient aluminum can that said Blatz on it. Rock pushed some chicken

34

bones and some newspapers off one easy chair, and sat down, raising a cloud of dust. He pried the lid of the can open and warm beer fizzed up. He took a slug. It wasn't very good, might *never* have been very good. But what the hell, it wet his whistle.

Archer opened his own can and drank it down in one long gulp. Then he wiped foam off his beard, burped, and said, "Good Beer!"

Rockson lied and agreed with Archer, adding, "Maybe you have some other brand? Just for variety?"

Archer went over and opened a picnic-type box made of styrofoam and took out a pair of dark old bottles. "Bass Ale," Archer said proudly. "I save for company. You like?"

"I'd love it," Rock said. Bass was his favorite, and glass bottles a hundred years old usually kept the taste better than cans of the same age! Rock accepted a chilled bottle — Archer had ice in the box — and leaned back and twisted the cap off. It fizzed and he drank it down. When he was done, he wiped the foam from his mouth as Archer had, and gasped out a long, heartfelt "Ahhhhh!"

They each had a few more, exchanging information about what had transpired over the years to each of them. The fire was dying by the time they had finished their updating, and Archer went to a pile of bowling pins jumbled in a corner and came back and fed ten or twelve pins into the fire.

"Aren't you lonely here?" Rock said.

"No," Archer replied. "Have good newspapers. Have lots of firewood. It not lonely here." His brow furrowed a bit, and Archer admitted, "But sometime miss old days — miss fighting Reds most! Miss trips to Russia on rocket ship! Ha! Remember me fly with you? Remember we prisoner in Soviet rocket?"

"Yeah I remember," Rock said, with a laugh. "I also seem to remember you farted up there in space and nearly killed everyone on board with the smell!" That particular reminiscence brought laughter from the giant.

When he stopped laughing, he added, "Sometimes visi-

35

tors drop by."

"Visitors?"

"You will see," Archer promised. "Nice visitors! Sometimes wild women come! Great-looks-women! They all alone, woman-alone tribe! Want to get pregnant! And me help them." The giant laughed again, rubbing his big barrel belly. Archer gave Rock a brief description of these "good-looks-women." From his friend's description of the women, Rockson concluded that he had been visited by the green-skinned wild women tribe that Rock had encountered once. They were called the Barbarahs, after their leader. They worshipped Barbarah as a goddess. And Barbarah demanded that they live apart from men, except to find one from time to time so the tribe could procreate.

"Those women could be dangerous," Rock cautioned his big friend. "Be careful."

"Me careful!" Archer said. "But they be great in sack! I have other visitor right now," Archer said. "You will see him. Just after kill bad men, find hungry dying man out on old road. He stay here get healthy on food I make!"

"Where is he?"

"I'm right here," someone said in a high, small voice from over by the bowling alley door. Rockson spun around, his hand on his pistol. There was a tiny thin man in a red tunic and curled-front red slippers standing there, smiling. The man said, "Hi. I'm Zydeco Realness. Who are you?"

Rockson told him and the little man gasped. The man's tiny green eyes lit up and he rushed over and shook Rock's hand. He didn't have much of a grip. "You are the great Doomsday Warrior! You are the man who saved America!"

Rockson let go of the butt of his gun. "Well . . . sort of."

"Glad, so glad to meet you! Excitement only diminished by tiredness factor. Understand? Sustenance necessary to restore health, comprehend?"

"Yes, I do." Rockson stared at the diminutive figure intently. The elf-man wore no weapons. He had a long,

36

pointy nose, high cheekbones, and a tiny goatee. He looked a hell of a lot like the little missile silo-dweller people Rockson had encountered some years back. The ones called—"Are you a Technician?" Rockson asked.

Zydeco Realness replied, "In a way. My people, like the so-called Technicians race you speak of, live in old missile silos. Living underground for so long affected our bodies in much the same ways as in that race you speak of now. But the Technicians, I so comprehend, are all dead now. Far as I equate. My people call themselves the Techno-survivors. And I am very happy-glad-pleased to meet you!" The little man again shot out a hand to shake Rockson's. It felt like a small, cold, child's hand, Rock decided.

"How long have you been here?"

"About a week now. I was very sick," the little man said as he helped himself to a Blatz, "but this magical relaxing liquid refreshment restored me!" He smiled a pointy-toothed grin and sat down on a hassock, popping open the can and sipping at it. "I traveled far to bring good news to Archer. We knew of him for years, we know of Century City, and all the guerrilla wars—everything—for years. We monitored broadcasts from our sealed missile silos. We decided to open up to world outside once we heard over wavelengths that, happiness-joyously-wonderful, there is at last peace. Techno-survivors have a high level of science. We make many things and we decided in meeting to offer such things as we make to the other Americans. Americans like you and Archer. I set out to bring word to nearest American who live on surface—Archer. But I'm not used to cold, to wind. I get very sick. I almost didn't make it."

"Glad you did," Rockson said. "What sort of things are you Techno-survivors manufacturing? Do you want to trade them for some of Century City's goods? If so I—"

"No! No trade. These things we make are gifts to you to show appreciation for finally winning war with Red Soviets! We eager, will return favor to great American patriots. I have a gift for you Rockson, for all American heroes. Not here—too big to bring. You and Archer will come see it in

Cavetown. Not far. Two days by foot-walking!"

"What is it?"

"Technical description has no equivalent. Device NQ-27364JTY is utterly new, and fun too. But best fun for dying men-heroes. Thing-device is ultra-goody-good for life's last days."

Rockson was pretty confused now. A fun thing for the dying? Is that what the Techno-survivors invented? "I don't have a hell of a lot of time, Zydeco," Rock said. "I should go back to my home. Maybe I can send someone from Century City to fetch it from your Cavetown. Give me the directions, I'll tell the city council and—"

"No," Zydeco insisted, the tip of his long nose starting to turn red. "You come and get it. *Now!* We don't like to be *dissed!* Warning. Last people that dissed us, are evaporated-gone-deceased-eliminated. Sorry!"

"Dissed?"

"Disrespected us," Zydeco said. "One thing we Techno-survivors can't stand, it's being dissed. I tell my people you don't accept nice gift, they might shoot a few old missiles at your city! Truth-veracity-sincerity."

"Are you threatening me?"

The little man's face turned pale. "No, I am not. That would be dissing you! I tell it like it is. Accept gift, then we friends. Friends forever." Zydeco's tiny voice had grown hoarse and tight. "Please don't make me tell them you dissed us!"

Rockson thought for a moment. The little man's people had missiles; that could be dangerous. Why not play along, accept his goddamned gift and avoid trouble? . . . Rock decided, said, "OK, Zydeco. I won't diss you! I will go and accept your present." He turned to Archer, who had been following the discussion as best he could. "You want to come with me, Arch?"

"Me come!"

As they packed supplies for the overland trip, Rockson

learned a little more about Device NQ-whatever-the-hell-it-was. Zydeco explained that it was a sort of dreaming chamber. You lay a man or woman who was dying inside it, press a button, and they dreamed their way into slumber with beautiful, happy dreams. Enjoyment instead of pain.

"Better to die that way," Zydeco said, beaming with his pointy teeth showing. They were greenish, a lighter tint than his little eyes.

"Yes, I guess so," Rock replied. But he, for one, would rather die the old-fashioned way, even if it hurt a lot. He would rather leave life conscious and aware of his death. Still, Rockson had to admit there were many casualties of the radiation leak back at C.C. who were living out their last days in terrible pain. Some of them might wish to use the machine.

"Cavetown," Zydeco said, "lies fifty miles due south."

"If the device is heavy, how do I get it to C.C.?" Rock asked.

"Antigravity stuff lifts it off ground," Zydeco explained. "I didn't leave it behind because it is heavy, but because it is our custom that giftee come accept gifts from us."

"Terrific," Rockson muttered under his breath. Sometimes he hated the customs of the various peoples he encountered in his far-flung journeys. So much rigmarole. He hated rigmarole!

It was around midnight before they had packed what they needed. "No walking at night," Zydeco said. "Too cold."

Rockson agreed. "OK," Rock said, "we can leave at dawn. After a good night's sleep." He yawned. "Where's the bed, Archy-boy?"

"I will have *them* show you!" Archer laughed and rang a dinner bell.

Out of a side room paraded a bevy of the loveliest and most scantily clad maidens Rockson had seen in a coon's age. Five green-skinned young wild-women! Their catlike yellow eyes flickered with lust, their tongues rolled over their lips.

"Hellcats in bed," Archer laughed. "Smell like lollipop!"

"Yeah, I know," Rock said, remembering his last tryst with one of these women. The deep scratch lines on his back had taken months to heal. But it *had* been—interesting.

Zydeco sighed audibly. "I will take three Blatz super-nutrition-liquids to bed with me for energy! Fun is ability divided by quotient of energy!" The little man went and got three of the old cans from the cabinet and disappeared, with a pair of the green-girls, into a side room. They towered over the little man, but he didn't seem bothered by that—nor did they.

The tallest and slinkiest wild-woman caught Rock's admiring eye. She approached, and pressed her warm, slithery, green body against him and her silvery blue, long hair slid across his cheek. She began an erotic dance, pushing her groin into his crotch. The subtle approach.

Rock, despite himself, felt his manhood stiffen. "Aw what the hell," he mumbled and took her around the waist. "Where's my room Arch?"

Archer laughed and pointed, as the last two women put their arms about the mountain man's massive waist. Rock and the wild-woman went into the side room and shut the door. There was a Coleman lamp lit in there, and a mattress on the floor, covered with a patchwork quilt that didn't look too dirty. Plus a case of Bass Ale. At least there was no garbage in the room. Archer Inn. Honeymoon hotel!

She started tearing at his clothes even before Rock had sunk down onto the quilt. He reached over and grabbed a bottle and took a swig, then just lay back and enjoyed it.

Chapter Five

Rock yawned widely, opened his eyes, and looked over to where the wild-woman had been, next to him on the bed. The dent on the pillow from her head was still there, but she was gone. He hadn't heard her leave — she had been very silent about it.

He sat up and stretched, his hands up high. That's when he felt the smart of a series of scratches on his muscular back. "Goddamned she-cat," he hissed. He put on his pants and undershirt and staggered into the main room, desperate for some coffee. Archer was already there, sitting at the sofa, slurping down a cup of java he had brewed. The smell hit Rockson's nostrils. *"Fresh* coffee!" he exclaimed. "Where the hell did you get it?"

"Wild-women bring," Archer replied tersely. Rock noticed that the mountain man was in his long johns, but he still had his weather-beaten, wide-brimmed leather hat jammed down on his head. Maybe he slept with it on! "Well, how about you give me a mug of that stuff," Rock demanded. As soon as he downed the cup that Archer poured from a battered percolator set over on a small, propane-fired camping stove in the corner, Rock asked, "Are all the women gone?"

Archer nodded. "They no stick around. But leave presents." He yawned like a bear. And his breath was like a bear's too.

"Where's Zydeco?" Rock asked.

Before Arch could answer, the little elf-man came out of his own room, wearing a candy-eating happy grin. "Great experience!" he exclaimed. "Excellent physical abilities. Good energy levels! Energy is product of

41

ratio of—"

"*Yeah,*" Rock said derisively, again feeling the scratches smart on his back, "and good fingernails too! Sit down Zydeco, and have a mug. After coffee we'll set off for that Cavetown of yours. It's a long walk so—"

"No walk," Archer smiled, putting down his cup. "Women leave mounts as presents. Three mounts! We ride!"

"Great," Rock said, meaning it this time. "What kind of horses are they?"

"They not horses."

"Oh—mules? Donkeys?"

"Come see!" Archer said, laughing.

They put down their cups and Archer led them into the blinding light of morning. There was a coating of frost on the ground and their breath came out in white clouds. Rockson and Zydeco had put on their boots, but Archer just walked in his holey old brown and stiff socks. The cold didn't seem to bother his size-twenty feet a bit.

When they had come around to the other side of the bowling center's main building, Rock saw the three mounts they were to ride—and gasped. "They're ostriches!" he exclaimed.

"Not exactly," Zydeco said, in pleased tones. "They are much better than that! I believe these mounts are Guam rail birds. Very large ones. Women-tribe uses them."

The seven-foot-high birds had their bridles tethered to a fallen branch under a bare tree. They turned their long necks and gazed suspiciously at the three men. The plumage of the birds was multicolored, like peacocks'. But the birds were shaped more like quails.

"Nice saddles," Rock said, seeing silvery embossed edging on the tawny leather saddles. He approached the birds slowly and they seemed to back off.

Zydeco said, "I saw the wild-women come here a few days ago riding some of these birds—with a few spares along. They told me it's important to smile when you approach the birds. Show no fear. Otherwise they can bite you—or kick you with their big taloned feet. They're very tough-rough-mean birds. They're descended, I believe, from some smaller of their species that escaped from zoos during the Nuke War. Those saddles are put on once. They stay on. They don't mind the saddles."

"Can they take Archer's weight?" Rock asked, somewhat dubious of any *bird's* ability to carry the oversized mountain man. Archer's feet would brush the ground, even if he sat on the saddle of the tallest bird.

"They can carry us easily," Zydeco said. He went over to one of the birds, smiling broadly and making cooing noises. The elf-man picked up a tuft of grass and fed it to the huge-beaked, tall bird, which took it and nuzzled against his tiny face. The bird's red beak was bigger than the elf-man's head. "Archer will get this big one. She likes mountain men, don't you Maha?" The bird seemed to nod, and then leaned into his caress, and he gave her some more grass. "Your bird is called Zaza, Rockson. And my baby is Mumu."

Archer ran back to fetch some clothing and lock up.

When Archer returned, Rockson said, "Come on. Let's mount up." The Doomsday Warrior, though he'd walked boldly toward the *meanest* of men, approached the second bird, Zaza, with the utmost caution, smiling as broadly as he could manage. Zydeco shouted out a series of pops and wheezes and the Guam rails, or whatever the hell they were called, squatted down, like they were sitting on eggs. Zydeco said, "Just like camels, the birds bend down for the rider to more easily mount them."

"Here goes nothing," Rock said. He did as Zydeco instructed, throwing his small pack of supplies up around the bird's thick neck. The supply bag hung there like a necklace. Then he scrambled up into the soft leather saddle. A few feathers fluffed off the bird's molting neck, and one stuck in his nose.

"Don't sneeze," Zydeco cautioned as Rockson rubbed it away. "They go mad if you sneeze. Remember, never-never-never sneeze."

"Just great," Rockson mumbled under his breath. He gingerly took the reins of the bird and once she stood up he said, "Giddy-yap, Zaza."

Nothing happened. Zydeco emitted a little, high-pitched giggle. "You say, 'Terp-terp!' " And with those words, his bird, Mumu, turned toward where he pulled the bridle and set off at a trot. Rock's and Archer's mounts followed suit. Soon they couldn't even see the bowling center. Rock figured they were making about twenty miles per hour. The ride was smooth and rolling, almost dreamlike. Occasionally a feather or two would dislodge and sometimes tickle at his nose. And he daren't sneeze!

The birds ran like pigeons, their necks jerking forward as if they were attached to the bumpy-skinned legs. They were ungainly but fast.

The adventurers traversed rolling grasslands for a while. Then the flat, frozen turf gave out onto a desert plain scattered with red-leafed pine shrubs. "How do you know where we're going?" Rock shouted over to Zydeco. "Are you following some landmarks? Do you have a compass?"

Zydeco's reply was nearly whipped away by the wind: "We Techno-survivors . . . innate sense of direction . . ." It would have to do as an explanation. The birds were running flat out now on the hard surface. Rock estimated that they were making about a hundred miles per hour! The wind was icy—good thing Archer had provided him with a parka!

After they rode for another hour, a rolling mist, scented with something that must have been decayed carcasses, came at them.

"Just a warm front," Zydeco called over to Rockson. "These Guam rails can see in fog; we don't have to slow down." Rock nodded but he felt that queer warning prickle on the nape of his neck that meant danger. This time it was *definite*.

They rode on at breakneck speed into the whiteout-solid mists. Rock hoped whatever the danger his sixth sense was detecting would be quickly skirted.

Not so.

Suddenly, the mist thickened and became dark as obsidian. They slowed down all of a sudden. Even the birds' keen infrared detecting eyes couldn't make things out in all this denseness. The birds seemed to shiver, as if they were cold. Or afraid. Zydeco clicked out some commands to the mounts. The shivering stopped.

Then the sounds came echoing in the darkness. Sounds like a thousand castanets being shaken. Rockson knew that sound. Snakes! Big rattlers made that sound. They were very near; a whole nest of them! But with all the echoes in the mist, it was hard to tell where the snakes were.

"Hey, do these birds fly?" Rockson asked hopefully.

Zydeco's reply was, "I wish."

Rockson quickly had his shotpistol out, and was pointing it at his best guess of where the rattlers were. A wind stirred the mists and the view before him turned from utterly black to dark gray. And he saw them. A hundred writhing diamond back sidewinders, sliding their angry way over the hard-packed soil. Rockson was about to fire—he had reloaded the shotpistol with the last of his ammo back at the bowling center. Archer too had his weapon out—the good old shotgun. Somehow, it didn't seem like enough.

"Put the guns away," Zydeco said. "And hold on tight, very tight to your saddles and the reins." He whispered out some bird-command words, and the Guam rails leapt suddenly into the air. They didn't fly, but they sure the hell could jump! Rockson realized that Zydeco was trying to have the birds hop right over the snakes, bound out of the area of danger. He jammed his boots into the stirrups and wrapped the reins triple around his hands, doing his best to keep from sailing off the mount.

But it didn't work. When the megabirds came down, they were right in the middle of a circle of writhing, ten-foot-long, pissed-off snakes. Out of the frying pan into the fire!

The Guam rails panicked and started shivering and shaking. The birds made whiny sounds, as if they were scared shitless. And all that shaking shook off clouds of itchy, twitchy feathers. Rockson got one jammed into his nostrils and he did what he had been told *not* to do — he sneezed!

That sneeze triggered a sudden insanity in the birds, just as Zydeco had cautioned it would. The birds lost their fear and squawked and jumped around as if someone had put a branding iron to the voluminous asses. Their fear was gone, replaced by a manic rage. The birds' talons dug into snake bodies, they jumped and kicked and pecked at the snakes, oblivious to the many venomous strikes against them. They also tried to throw their riders. More feathers flew, and Rockson, and Archer too, gave out terrible *AAACHHOOOOSS!* That kept the birds crazy.

Rock was glad for wearing his boots, as several sharp rattler-jabs hit his toes. The frenzied action went on for a minute or more, the riders holding on like rodeo riders in a rodeo of death. The snakes, suddenly, were the ones in danger. They were being torn into mincemeat by the furious birds. It was all Rockson could do to hold onto his seat.

Then it was over, over as fast as it had begun. There were nothing but torn-open snakes below the birds' bloody toes, and the rest of the rattlers were sliding away into the mists. The birds simmered down. Rockson tried and succeeded in not repeating his sneezing fit, although fluff was everywhere in the misty air. Rockson took a deep breath. He wasn't sure he had

46

even breathed the whole time the incredible thing was happening.

"Anyone hurt?" Rockson asked. But he could see no one was hurt. Archer was still in the saddle; the giant mountain man hadn't even let go of his twenty-gallon leather hat. And Zydeco was still atop Mumu. The elf-man was pallid, but otherwise looked all right. God knows they'd have been dead a thousand times over if they had fallen off their kill-mad mounts. At Rock's urgent suggestion, Zydeco gave a set of commands to the birds, who turned and started to run in the direction opposite the remaining snakes. Soon they were out of the near-opaque mists, and once again into bright sunlight. Rock rode alongside his companions neck and neck. It was as if the birds were running for the finish line in a strange Kentucky Derby.

"We must be going one eighty!" Rock shouted.

Both Zydeco and Archer laughed. Zydeco's laugh was a high-pitched, tinny, elf laugh, a strange mad cackle that increased in volume as he took the lead.

Chapter Six

The bird-riders were dusty and worn by the time they came upon the great cliff of caves at dusk. The orange beams of low sunlight illuminated a deep darkness in one of the rock faces immediately before them. "That's Cavetown—up there." Zydeco announced. "Come on, I'm sure they have seen us approach. Let me go ahead first, so the guards don't ray us down. They don't expect me to come back on top of a Guam rail bird. We Techno-survivors have had trouble with renegade bands of Russians once in a while. The Red deserters roam as bandit marauders in this area of Utah."

"Russians?" Rock unclipped his shotpistol holster. All the Russian soldiers were supposed to be off American soil, but the Sov government had lost contact with some of its far-flung Special Forces. The bastards were worse than sidewinders.

Zydeco saw Rock move toward his pistol and said, "Don't worry! The Reds haven't bothered us this year at all. Let's get inside and have some sustenance!"

"I'm for that—and a nice cold beer, right Arch?" Rock added. "Bring on the Blatz!"

Archer just shook his head up and down emphatically. Rockson thought the big man's bird was looking a little the worse for wear. He felt sorry for anyone that had to carry the megapound moose-man on his back.

Their strange mounts plunged on after Zydeco, up a dusty ramp and into the darkness of a huge cavern. Inside they saw no one for a while. Then, from a hundred hiding places pairs of tiny yellow and green eyes appeared. As the eyes moved forward, huge banks of lights came on in the high ceiling.

Rock gasped. It was a vast chamber filled with equipment, populated by several scores of men and women much like his elfish companion. The Techno-survivors were dressed in tunics, the women — cute, little long-haired pixies with pointy noses and red cheeks — wearing also short skirts. Some of their outfits were red, some orange, some yellow or green. It probably denoted rank, or job specialty, Rock decided. They were chittering away to one another as the riders moved along into the center of the cavern and dismounted. All around Rock and his friends, bizarre plastic and metallic shapes loomed, machines of incomprehensible scientific functions.

After they dismounted, a man in a white tunic — the only one in a white tunic — came over to Zydeco and raised a hand, palm forward. "Greetings and undeserved happiness, Zydeco-citizen," he said.

Zydeco bowed slightly and said, "And I, noble surgeon Escadrille, am giving you the same."

The noble surgeon, who had silver gray locks, turned to look at Zydeco's towering companions and asked Zydeco, "Have either of these outlanders *dissed* you?"

"No, they are honorable," Zydeco replied.

Only then did the chief surgeon smile at Rockson and give him and Archer fond greetings, which Rockson returned as best he could. He wondered if the little ray gun hanging on the surgeon's side would have been drawn on him if Zydeco had told the elder that Rockson had "dissed" anyone. Rockson had no doubt that a ray from that tiny gun could do bad things to a man! The level of science indicated by the machines in this cavern betokened great power — to harm or to help. No dissing allowed!

Together with Escadrille, they went over to a long plasti-wood conference table. Archer was seated at one end, and Rock at the other, as honored guests. A long line of little people paraded by, the pixie-women curtsy-

49

ing to the visitors, the men shaking their hands. Some of the awed populace asked for Rock's autograph, and he obliged, borrowing a funny soft-tip pen.

They were served some green, odd-shaped but tasty fruit, some dry but peppery bread, and some vintage wine. Then came a main course, sizzling hot meat buns — probably deer meat. The buns were very small and Archer liked them very much. He gobbled them down with swigs of the wine. The server-girls brought more whenever Archer finished a pile. They were piled so high at one point that Rock couldn't see Archer behind the buns! But that was only for a short time. Archer quickly ingested the pile. A tremendous burp issued from the mountain man's lips, and as he turned red, all those within earshot — and that was most of the populace — laughed. Archer laughed too, an echoing rumble like an earthquake.

Once they finished the vast repast, business began: the business of accepting an unwanted, if interesting, gift. Rock was told he was free to examine the "Dream Machine" any time he wanted.

"How about now?" Rockson was more curious than a cat.

Zydeco and the chief surgeon walked over to the south side of the cavern, which was the point farthest from the entrance. A rectangular object lay on the rock-tiles there. It was waist high and about seven feet long by three feet wide. It was covered by a tarpaulin. "My invention," Escadrille said, proudly.

Zydeco pulled the cover off and Rockson and Archer got a look-see. The device that had prompted the long, grueling ride across the wastelands looked very much, Rockson thought, like a so-called iron lung of the bad old twentieth century — a leftover of the awful polio epidemic days. In short, it was a little scary looking. Rockson had seen some cryogenic tanks in Century City's science labs that had a not dissimilar appearance as well. The tanks were used to freeze-dry live animal and plant lab specimens for later awakening and study.

The surgeon described the principles of the dream machine thusly: "The body in question lies down in the device, and then the electromechanical servo-systems slow that body's functions all down. The low rate of pulse and nutrient feeding necessary to maintain a body in stasis—alive and well, in perfect balance—is maintained automatically. Attachments to the brain are effected, tiny connectors that keep the brain on a normal level of alertness. But all stimuli come not from the outside, but from programmed-in experience modules. Understand?"

"A bit," Rock said, while Archer just looked blank.

The surgeon frowned, and opened the full-length lid of the device. Inside was like the inside of a coffin, nice and comfy and silken. Rock had no desire to lie in there.

As if reading Rockson's thoughts, Zydeco said, "It is best to demonstrate the device. Why don't you get inside, Rock, and take it for a spin? Have a nice dream—for just a short period."

Rockson must have looked dubious, for the surgeon added, "It is perfectly safe, let me assure you. Don't diss me, stranger."

"I'm *sure* it is safe," Rock said, "but how do you set it? What kind of dream will it be set on? How long will I be in there? I want to make the trip as short as possible."

"Ah, good questions," the surgeon said, smiling. He pointed out a mass of dials and lights on the side of the box. "As for how the device is set: these controls are microchip circuits. We improvised many circuits out of old missile guidance systems, and added some new things. You can look at the blueprints later. As for your second question, you will have a very pleasant dream, as the device is set to plumb your own mind for imagery and dream-personnel. It will probably be a rather—er—sensual dream—if you wish. Of course, we can also create dreams for you from scratch. We have a list of generic off-the-shelf dreams. You know: playboy, soldier in victorious action, all that sort of stuff.

"The dream will seem to take an hour, but you will only be inside the device for five minutes. Hardly a waste of your precious time!" The surgeon glared at Rockson. "You're not dissing me, are you? You like the present, don't you?"

He hoped he wouldn't have to put up with this "diss" stuff much longer! Rockson nodded, mumbling, "Love it. Can't wait to haul it home!" But he thought other, less happy thoughts. He didn't like having gifts crammed down his throat.

"Me try nice dream too?" Archer asked. "Make me dream of women. Very long, very nice dream!"

Zydeco frowned. "Sorry, Archer. We don't have a box big enough for you — yet. We'll work on it," Zydeco laughed. "Now, how about it, Rockson?"

He was a little wary, so Rock whispered to Archer, "If anything seems wrong, get me outta there." Then Rockson got into the "coffin" and the lid closed over him with an ominous hiss. Zydeco leaned over the face plate and told Rock, "We'll set it on a five-minute ride, pleasure sequence."

Rock nodded and closed his eyes, though he wasn't sure that was necessary. Small suction cups on the ends of copper wires crawled out of the sides of the device and attached to his forehead with a mild thump.

"Bon voyage, Rockson," the chief surgeon smiled through the suddenly foggy face plate.

Rockson found himself suddenly spinning around, as if going underwater, or into a dream. He was soon seeing a different place entirely than the Techno-survivor's cavern. He was lying in a magnificent bed, inside a palatial apartment in old New York City. The bed was next to a floor-to-ceiling window. Below him, glittering with starlike lamp lights, was a darkened Central Park.

And suddenly he didn't know that he was dreaming. He was aware that he had awakened *from* a dream, however. Something of an odd dream about a cave . . . but that dream faded away rapidly. He was Niles Rockson, famous playboy, and this was his apartment. And he was not alone in the silken sheets of his luxurious, heart-shaped bed!

He was lying next to a beautiful woman. Her name was Kimetta, and she was the beautiful, strawberry blond daughter of a delegate to the United Nations. Rockson had wined and dined the lusty beauty the night before. And now she moaned, turned over, and wrapped her arms around him. Kimetta wanted to make love again, and he was more than ready.

As Rock dreamed on, there was a sudden commotion in the cavern. Rays of blue fire shot out from several guardposts near the cavern entrance. Fire returned *fivefold* by the attacking forces of Soviet irregulars! Archer raced to the table where he had left his shotgun, and raised it, intending to go and help out the guards, who had raised a general alarm. Then he hesitated, and instead ran back to the box wherein his friend lay sleeping. Zydeco and the surgeon had rushed away. And Archer didn't know what to do. He was supposed to rouse Rockson if something bad happened. But *how* did you get the box open?

He looked for a hinge or a knob and found none. Blue rays that seemed to melt walls of granite and flesh just as easily flashed overhead. And bullets flew also. The screams increased in intensity, mad high-pitched screams of Techno-survivors being hit by the intense fire. The defenders were losing, dying like flies.

As Archer fumbled with the coffinlike container,

trying to get Rockson out, the Soviets came into his immediate area. Hundreds of grim-faced commandos poured from every direction, several training their guns upon Archer. He dropped the insignificant shotgun. He had to surrender, for he feared wild shots would hit the dream machine! He raised his hands.

Then the Sov's rotund, filthy-uniformed commander, General Mikael Zhabnov, stepped forward. Zhabnov! One of Archer's old enemies. Archer, unable to contain himself, lunged at him, but was hit instantly with a blue ray. It didn't kill him, it was just a low energy stun blast. After the mountain man toppled, the general approached, turned over Archer's inert form with a big boot, and smiled. "I know this man!"

The general couldn't have been more pleased. His men had been on a slave-hunting expedition when they had found the interesting cavern. The devices in here looked *very* interesting. The little people must be very smart. Zhabnov's renegades could use some very smart slaves. After all, Zhabnov had a fortress to build, a world to win. That's why he had instructed his troops, once the upper hand was achieved, to reduce the level of charge in their ray weapons, to stun rather than kill. They needed slaves for labor. This wretched-smelling mountain man would be a very strong slave! And he would be treated very badly, for Zhabnov hated the man. Nearly as much as he hated Archer's famous boss—the Doomsday Warrior. He looked around, nervous that another of the famed Free-fighters might be lying in hiding nearby.

He saw a box that looked like a coffin, only made of metal. "See what that is," he told one of his lieutenants, Zimski. Zimski ran over and peered down into a small window on the box. "A body inside," he said. "Guy is blue—and not breathing."

"Well, then he won't bother us. Come back here and start supervising the rounding up of new slaves. Tie them all up well before they awaken. Be especially careful not to bruise the pretty little women!" Zhabnov's jowls twitched in pleasure as he added, "Tie this giant up, too, before he awakes and kills some of you." Then the puffy-lipped general strode triumphantly to a high platform. He stepped over the inert forms of several red tunic-clad elves lying on the stairs as he ascended to the top of the platform. He faced forward, jaw jutting out like Mussolini's, and announced to the few Techno-survivors left standing disarmed before his troops, "This place is now the property of the New Soviet World State." (This was the general's rather vainglorious misnomer for his tiny separatist movement.) "Where is Rockson? Where are the other Free-fighters? The giant known as Archer cannot be alone here! Speak up and you shall be rewarded."

No one answered. Zhabnov rubbed his bushy black eyebrows, a habit he had developed that signified he was about to have a brilliant thought. As a matter of fact, he seemed to have a light bulb burst in his mind. Rockson . . . he was *always* with Archer . . .

The Coffin! *Who* was in the coffin? Had he interrupted some sort of funeral? Was the blue-faced man in the box his nemesis, Rockson?

Chapter Seven

Zhabnov ran down off the platform and brushed past the startled first rank of renegade officers toward the coffin. He bent his flabby body over the face plate and tried to make out the face he saw inside it. And he gasped aloud. "It *is* Rockson! I knew that the giant mountain man's presence indicated that his leader, Rockson, had to be nearby. But he's dead! Remarkable! And sad . . ." Zhabnov stood up and seemed about to shed a tear. "I had *so* hoped to find and torture Rockson! So sad that he is dead!" His officers stood uneasily, awaiting orders.

"But . . . what a strange coffin . . ." Zhabnov felt along the lid. It was cold, colder by far than the cavern itself. And all those wires, all that electrical cabling feeding into the coffin. Could it be that it was some kind of suspended-animation chamber? Could it be that his luck was great this day? Could it be that Rockson was *not* dead? Zhabnov swung around and looked at the small band of little men and women that had been rounded up. "Who knows about this box? Who is a physician among these little shits?"

The older elf in the white lab-smock seemed to shuffle a bit on his little red slippers, and Zhabnov smiled. "Ah, yes, *you!* Come over here! What is this box?"

Lieutenant Zimski pushed the little fellow forward until he was almost touching Zhabnov's distended stomach. Zhabnov grabbed the man up by his lapels and hoisted him in the air. The physician was feather light. "OK, doctor, spill!"

Twisting the surgeon's arm, Zhabnov shortly made him reveal the true nature of the device that held the sleeping Doomsday Warrior. And General Zhabnov was fascinated — and pleased. "So," Zhabnov said, wiping his

56

pudgy fingers over his four o'clock shadow. "So the box is a dream machine? How truly remarkable."

"What shall we do with this little doctor?" Zimski asked. "Shall we take him out to the truck with the other slaves, or shoot him right here?"

"No! Don't kill him. I need him to operate this device. A dream machine can become a nightmare machine, I think, with a little rewiring!"

"I won't do it," the little, white-smocked man protested. But after Zhabnov's torture experts applied a device called the "compressor" to the little doctor's head, he was very willing to cooperate.

The reprogramming of the dream machine began.

Niles Rockson, millionaire man about town, playboy sought after by all the loveliest women in the world, had just finished making love to the sensual, oh-so-desirable Kimetta. Now, as she brushed away at her long, silken, strawberry blond hair at the Louis XIV dressing table mirror, Rockson sat up in his silk bedsheets and stretched. He saw that dawn was breaking over the park. All the little people, those without any *real* money, were hurrying around to go to their dull little jobs. They were living dull little lives. But not Rockson. No, his life of enjoyment and luxury went on and on, without any such thing as that ugly word *work* to interfere with his pleasures!

Rockson leaned over and extracted the bottle of Dom Perignon Champagne from its crystal decanter next to the bed. He poured himself another sparkling glass of the bubbly, sipped it slowly. There was a full breakfast, which his butler James had deposited right on the table next to the heart-shaped bed, once Kimetta had slipped into her brocaded dressing gown. Now Rockson put down the champagne and put the silver spoon against the shell of one of the two-minute poached eggs. It was done just perfectly, as always, and so was the toast under the silver lid, still warm and with all the ugly crust cut off of it! And the marmalade! Superb!

When you were rich, young, and handsome, and lucky as well, life just got better and better, didn't it?

Kimetta came over to the bed. She sat there, her knees tucked under her. She took the silver spoon from his hand and said, "I'll feed you, darling." He lay back with his hands under his head on the satin pillows as she spoon fed him the poached eggs.

"You are the best lover, darling, absolutely the best," she cooed.

"So they *all* say," Rockson replied, in a jaded, I-couldn't-care-less way. He reached over and flicked on the multi-speaker stereo system, and sultry tropical rhythms coursed through the palatial bedroom suite.

After listening to the music a bit—music always turned on Kimetta—she put the breakfast aside, stood up, threw back her long locks and toyed with the ribbon-tie of her gown. "Can we make love again?" she pleaded.

Rockson nodded.

She sighed and slid out of the handmade silk and then came to him again. Naked she slipped under the sheets. Kimetta ran her long, cool fingers through his black-with-a-streak-of-white hair and kissed him furiously. He drew her to him. His shoulder, his neck, his cheek were covered with hot kisses.

She knew his anatomy like a map. Kimetta was like a well-tuned sports car riding down a familiar road. But this morning she was taking the express route to his fulfillment. His hands moved softly, expertly across the sumptuous plush curves of her desirable body. He lingered to cup her very full and ripe breasts, which seemed to swell to his touch. She moaned and her lips slid down his hairy chest.

"Darling," she moaned, "anything for you. How may I please you, now?" Rockson was just about to say—

And then . . . something went wrong, horribly wrong!

Slowly, ever so slowly, Rockson's pleasant interlude with Kimetta took an unpleasant turn. The room changed. Gone was the wide window with the beautiful view. It was replaced by a cracked old dusty window with a crooked, yellowed shade pulled almost all the way down to cover it. The Louis XIV dressing table became a wobbly-legged secondhand dinette table with a faded, imitation-wood plastic top. The mirror above it became dirty and clouded with age. Part of its frame was broken. The ceiling above became yellowed, and cracked, and much lower. There were flies stuck onto the crooked shade that half-concealed one bare electric bulb.

And Kimetta pulled away suddenly. She leaned away from the filthy brown encrusted sheets of the squeaky old lumpy daybed and said, "I hafta go to the john." Her lipstick was smeared, her hair dirty.

"W-what?" he mumbled. He closed his eyes, squeezed them tight. He must be hallucinating, Rockson decided. Yes, that was it, too much champagne. An hallucination. Maybe. But when Rockson opened his eyes again, it was the same. No, it was worse. In addition to the room looking like a hideout for a two-bit gunsel on the run, there was a smell. A god-awful, foul smell, like he was living in a backed-up cesspool. Rockson heard the john flush with an unpleasant gurgle and roar. Was it the damned toilet that smelled so bad? Could lovely sensual Kimetta lay such a — perish the thought!

Rockson reached over and delicately lifted the yellowed shade to peer outside. Gone was the spectacular view of Central Park. Instead—instead—

No it can't be.

There was a fetid swamp, its dead, rotted trees hung with long strands of Spanish moss-like growth. He let go of the shade and moaned. That foul smell was definitely coming in via the cracks of the window. What a stench—of human excrement and vegetable decay—like the sewers of Paris! What the hell was going on?

Kimetta started back from the bathroom. At least *she* looked about the same. Beautiful, long, and full. "Kimetta?" he asked, "where are we? What's going on? Am I dreaming?"

She laughed and said, "Wow! You really tied one on last night didn't you? Where the hell do you *think* we are? We're in your stinking home, that's where we are!"

She picked up an old dowdy housecoat and slipped it on, buttoning the one button that was still loosely clinging to the moth-eaten cloth. "Come on," she said, "let's finish off that bottle of rotgut for breakfast."

Rockson sat up, trying to pull himself together. Kimetta sat on the side of the bed and lifted a bottle of something purple called Rumple Town off the wooden floor. She placed it to her lips and drank down a slug, then, half choking, passed it to Rockson.

"I must be hallucinating," he mumbled, pushing the bottle away. "There's no other explanation. Where's my penthouse overlooking Central Park? Where's my great furniture?"

Kimetta nearly fell over laughing, and when she recovered she said, "Good God, loverboy, you can be really funny sometimes, I swear! You snap out of it now. And get your act together. This is your damned little shack, right smack in the middle of an overheated Venusian swamp!"

"Venusian? You mean I'm on the planet Venus?"

"You got it pal," Kimetta sneered. "This is your life, buddy. You asked for it, you know. You're the one that wanted to come here and 'find your fortune' and all that. And you dragged me along. But you ain't gonna live off of me no more. You're gonna work from now on pal. No more freeloading. That's what the new dictator said. That's what the law is now!" She took the bottle up again and drained it, letting some wine or whatever it was slip down her chin. Then Kimetta slipped on an old pair of beige slippers and headed for the door.

"Where are you going?"

"To get some more wine, you shitface. That is, if the bastard will still advance a bottle based upon us paying him next week."

"I — I don't understand what's going on," Rockson said. "Kimetta, can you come back here," he pleaded, "I'm having trouble this morning. . . . Can you tell me where my poached eggs are?"

"Poached eggs? Oh brother, you really are out of it aren't you?" She came back, but only to stand over him and sneer. "Now listen buster, it's one thing to be a failure, a bum, a no good exploiter of women, but it's another thing to be *bonkers*. I won't stay with no creepy flip-out, you know. If the captain's left the bridge, I'm outta here."

Rockson got mad now. How could she talk to him like this? He was a millionaire playboy! "Well," he huffed, throwing aside the dirty sheets and striding over to the closet where his wardrobe of suits should have been — only this closet looked kind of small — "you can very well leave me if you want! There are a hundred women dying to be here with me." He opened the closet and saw just one checkered sport coat, and a pair of soiled chino pants on a hook.

"Ha!" she laughed. "Maybe you were something back in the old days, but now you're a bum. No one else will have you, you freeloader! So you want me to leave you, heh? Well, when you pay me back for all the sex, for all the money you 'borrowed,' then I'll leave, and not until then! You think that you can just use me and then tell me to leave? Well, here on Venus there's laws about stuff like that! Sexual relations are sacred, buster. The man that has me has an obligation."

"I made no promises —," he started to say.

Kimetta stamped her bare feet. "You led me on! Well, I see I did right to report you! I hope they hang people like you. You — you destroyed my reputation."

Rockson's head swam. None of this was right. Something in the champagne was making him hallucinate. Surely that was it.

Kimetta, acting much like an angry tramp, threw things at him. He ducked. She continued to rave, adding, "Well, Mr. Cheapscrew, Mister Bigshot! I certainly don't want to play bed-doll with the likes of you anymore! I — I *hate* you!"

61

She reached onto a torn and faded stuffed chair's arm, and picked up some clothes. She started to put on a red blouse, and then an oddly shimmering, silver-materialed skirt. All the while, Kimetta kept yammering, giving him an awful headache: "You — you think women are your servants, your fuckin' concubines!" She spat at him, threw both of the slippers. He blocked the slippers with his arm, as he had the other debris she had hurled at him. They bounced against the headboard of the bed. Kimetta put on her alligator-skin stiletto-heeled pumps, then zipped up her skirt. She reached for the doorknob. But as she did so, there was an immense, insistent pounding at the door. The sound startled Rockson. For some reason he feared that kind of knock. Why? What did it mean?

Kimetta laughed. "Better put something on, buster. You know what that kind of knock means! Get dressed! We gotta open up."

Rockson whispered, "Hold your horses! Wait a damned minute." He threw on the chinos and the horrendous checkered sports jacket before she opened the door.

He knew exactly who they were by their uniforms and their shiny, arrogant faces. The Interplanetary Police, Venusian Sector Squad.

"What do you want?" Rock asked.

The fat jowly officer stepped forward, as his pair of assistants leveled guns at Rockson's gut. "Shut up, you woman abuser," the officer said. He slapped Rockson in the face.

The blow stung, and Rockson wanted to return it five-fold. But he knew he'd better not. He stood his ground, though. And he asked, "Why did you hit me? What is the meaning of coming here like this?"

Rockson could hardly make himself heard, for Kimetta was screaming. "It's about time you got him! Take him away! Take the shitface abuser away!"

The corporal — Rockson knew he was a corporal by the number of blue stripes on his gray uniform's epaulets — smiled. He said, "Ah, the gentleman doesn't yet know the charges against him? Well, I will tell you: You have committed the crime of playboyism, and the crime of borrowing money from women. And also the crime of putting liquor on a chit and then not paying. All these things are now crimes, effective . . . ," the corporal looked at his watch, "in two minutes! The freeloading scum of Venus are now subject to 'transport' for these crimes. Your criminal acts have been outlawed! Now, will you come peaceably, or should we pain-stun you?"

Rockson retorted, "Wait! Even if there's some new laws, they've just come into use, you say! So, if I don't do those illegal things anymore, you can't punish me for what happened before the new laws were passed!"

"There is also a new law making the new laws retroactive!" The captain glared from under bushy black eyebrows. "Now, you will come along. You are under arrest, which means you are guilty, and now you are condemned to transport off-planet!"

"Transport?" Somehow Rockson knew what that meant. And he paled. It meant going to a prison-asteroid. Forever.

Even Kimetta, who had just been so angry at Rockson, had gasped at that sentence. She paled and said, "So harsh . . . can't you give him one more chance? Even *he* doesn't deserve—"

"Silence," the officer cautioned. "You are the daughter of a man of influence, but I warn you not to interfere!" The fat man pushed Kimetta, and she fell back against the bureau, and her blouse opened to reveal one of her large, firm, and rounded breasts.

As the officer and the men with him gaped, Rockson saw his chance. He made a leap for the window, but as he crashed through the glass, a pain-stun blast shot out of the corporal's gun, and there was terrible searing pain. And then an utter darkness descended, like a heavy curtain.

Chapter Eight

General Mikael Zhabnov sat at the Techno-survivors' long conference table and ate the tiny buns that his unwilling hosts had prepared. He found the food that the elves — or whatever they were — served up was quite tasty. He was careful, however. He made one of them eat a few buns from the big serving dish from time to time. Just to make sure the little people weren't poisoning him.

As Zhabnov added calories to his already portly body, he watched his technicians working with the white-smocked surgeon Escadrille upon the opened and exposed control panel of Rockson's dream box. The surgeon had been tortured repeatedly to force his cooperation. And now that the secrets of the amazing dream device — as well as a few of his fingernails and teeth — had been extracted from the little man, the rewiring work was going at a good clip. Rockson's dream was being turned into a nightmare — an *endless* nightmare.

"Have you printed out the changes yet?" Zhabnov called over to the technicians at the coffinlike device.

One of his men, Tarlask, stood up, turned, and saluted. "Some of the printout is available for your perusal, excellency."

"Well then, come on! Give them to me! Let me see the results of the alterations to Rockson's dream program."

Zhabnov was disappointed when he was handed the accordion-fold paper from the technicians. It was all symbols, complicated computer jargon. He didn't have the slightest idea what it meant. So he put it down and said, "Tarlask, perhaps you will summarize this for me, I don't have much patience for lengthy reading. I don't have my reading glasses."

"Yes excellency!" the thin, gangly technician said, saluting. Then he proceeded to inform the general what the data from the printout meant: "Rockson's dream has changed from pleasant to most unpleasant. You can clearly see this from the spikes on pages three and seventeen, as you have noticed, have you not?"

"Most definitely," Zhabnov agreed, though he had no idea what all that mess of lines and arcs meant at all. "Now go on."

"Yes sir! Well, these wavy lines here show a constancy with the original character in his dream — we believe that the machine has created an ideal woman out of two women in Rockson's real life — for his enjoyment. That is, before we altered the wiring. *Now* that dream woman has become a betraying shrew — see these lines of disturbance on pages —"

"Yes, yes," Zhabnov said impatiently. He wondered how the hell Tarlask could read this stuff. But that's what he got paid for, wasn't it? Zhabnov did the planning, took care of the big thinking, the big picture. And Zhabnov's soldiers and technicians took care of the petty details! "Go on!"

Tarlask folded out more paper. "And on line twelve-oh-seven, you see, the location of the dream in space-time matrix has been moved from the time-place Rockson believes is an idyllic matrix — the late twentieth century in New York City, in a penthouse — to another matrix. Now these wavy and jagged lines combined show that the dream has been altered so that Rockson is now dreaming deeply that he is in a fetid swamp on Venus, and he has been arrested for a crime he didn't even know was an offense. We have," the technician's face grew a bit red, "introduced an arresting officer that is in appearance and behavior much like you, sir. Rockson's brain patterns contain a very in-depth description of his, er, interpretation of your personality. A most unfavorable one!"

"Yes . . ." Zhabnov beamed, "I see! Rockson is having a nightmare and I am in that nightmare, one of his torturers!"

"Exactly. If I may say so sir, you have an excellent grasp of science."

Zhabnov's chest swelled and a medal unclipped from his uniform, which he hastened to reattach. He stared at the half-finished pile of meat buns and decided perhaps he might be overdoing his repast. Then he brought his attention back to Tarlask. "Go on."

Tarlask said, "We are programming in a real shocker for Rockson now. He had been programmed to come out of the dream soon, but that has been changed. He will believe he is being transported to a prison-world far into space. We did this because his brain patterns show a dislike of outer space, and a positive repulsion for isolation and imprisonment."

Zhabnov smiled and said, "Good work, Tarlask! My compliments to the rest of your men. Make sure Rockson never comes out of that nightmare, can you do that?"

"Yes sir. We can have the nutrients and the other metabolic systems feed him inside that box for the next fifty years. He will grow old and die in that box, having an endless nightmare, just as you ordered."

"Rockson deserves worse," Zhabnov said in almost a hiss, "for all the trouble he has caused me. But, I am a compassionate man; this torture will do. Now finish your work and let us leave this unwholesome cave and its damp atmosphere with our bounty of new slaves. Make sure that giant mountain man is kept fully sedated, for I especially don't want him to know what we did to his leader. I will try to find as awful a fate for Archer."

Tarlask saluted and went back to his work.

And Zhabnov started eating meat buns again.

The surgeon's hands and his forehead were slippery with perspiration, despite the cool dampness of the cavern. Surgeon Escadrille had joined the mad Russian general's technicians in rewiring the dream-box. He had to do it. They not only tortured him, but his wife as well, and Zydeco's head was still pressed between two spike-boards. Whenever the surgeon seemed to slow in his work, the bastards would tighten the compressor-boards around Zydeco's head a bit more, and his friend would scream and scream.

The surgeon was in a desperate spot. He wanted to do something for the Doomsday Warrior, who lay blue-faced and shallowly breathing inside the dream machine-turned-torture device. But he had to make the printouts look *good* to the Soviets. Therefore the slight alterations Escadrille made in the reprogramming of the dream machine were minute. He hoped they would be enough to give Rockson a slim chance to get out of the nightmare, a slim chance to escape the endless hell they were preparing for him! But Escadrille wasn't sure. Heaven help Rockson!

He worked under the constantly glaring eyes of the Soviet scientists. It was only possible to make the little changes he *had to* make, in order to save Rockson, because the Sovs didn't always know what he was doing—his knowledge of his device far exceeded their abilities to understand.

The surgeon briefly obscured his hands with his body, and then made a slight change in the wires. Now, if he just moved this wire a bit over to *here,* and let this other wire feed into the primary circuit board via the second and not the first connector, so that there would be a loop in the current instead of a cross-circuit . . . There! Now there would be some faults in the program. Slight anomalies. Rockson might find that not *all* of his dream was a nightmare. He might find a door out!

Zhabnov yawned and glanced at his Tissot watch. His men had been rewiring Rockson's coffin of nightmares for five hours. Wasn't it completed yet? He got up, burped, and loosened his belt over his bulging stomach.

67

He went over to Tarlask, who, with two other Soviet technical officers and the white-smocked little man, was leaning over the circuit of the dream machine. Zhabnov said, "Well, isn't the job done yet?"

Tarlask stood up and said, "We're just about to close up the panel board, excellency. The job is almost done."

"Good. It is time to leave." The general shouted out, "Get ready to move out. Make sure all the slaves are loaded on the transport truck. Take all the equipment we labeled to be removed. Don't forget those weird, huge birds."

His men started running around and packing up their spoils of war and Zhabnov watched the panel being screwed back into place on the nightmare coffin. He looked into the frosty face plate at Rockson's blue face. Was that an expression of pain on his lips? Yes . . . Zhabnov was sure that expression was different. The nightmare was getting a bit rough no doubt. And it would get rougher. Lost in a reverie, Zhabnov thought, "I did it! I have killed Rockson—or rather I have set up a torture that will end in his wasting away in this box. I'm greater than Colonel Killov! I have succeeded where that bastard has failed. It is I, not Killov, who survived and destroyed Rockson. Again, that is another proof that it is *my* destiny to rule the world! I will build up my forces, invent new weaponry with the assistance of these tiny but brilliant Techno-survivors. I will soon oust that black usurper Rahallah from the Kremlin, personally roll the wheelchair containing my senile uncle Premier Vassily down that magnificent flight of stairs in the Winter Palace . . . Let's see. Where shall I have *my* capital? Washington? Moscow? No! Someplace *warm,* someplace suitable for my old age. Maybe Mexico. Yes, I shall be the new Montezuma!

Zhabnov stood there above Rockson's box and laughed softly for a long while. Tarlask, looking confused and worried, touched his master's shoulder. "Sir? You alright, sir?"

"Eh?" Zhabnov pulled himself back to reality. "Yes. I was thinking, that's all. It's—nothing! Let's get out of here!" And then Zhabnov smiled crookedly. "But first, Tarlask, go out to my vehicle and bring me one of the American Beauty roses in the freezer-compartment."

"W-what color rose is that sir? There are so many types of wonderful roses that you have raised, as you know sir and—"

"Idiot! You call yourself a scientist? You don't know a *thing* about roses, though, do you?"

"N-no sir!"

"Well, they are *red!* And large petaled! Oh, just ask the chauffeur. He will show you! Bring that rose back at once."

The thin scientist ran off to comply with the order. Zhabnov just stared at Rockson's tortured expression until the technical man returned with the long-stemmed rose. He took it from the lackey and placed it atop Rockson's coffin, just below the face plate, and said, "This for you, Rockson. A parting gift. An American Beauty rose, just for you." He turned and started to walk away from Rockson. Zhabnov was the last one in the cavern, he realized. No one was around. No one.

And Zhabnov had an impulse he couldn't resist. He went back to the coffin, leaned over, and stared at Rockson's face again. "You look so peaceful, like sleeping beauty," Zhabnov whispered. And he planted a fat wet kiss on the glass.

A short time later, Zhabnov peered out of the periscope of his converted RV command vehicle. He was looking back at the cavern's wide, dark opening and anticipating a wonderful sight. Zhabnov could hear the wails of the little people as they awakened in the large transport truck that rumbled along beside his vehicle. They wouldn't like being slaves very much, but they would get used to it. Used to obeying orders. And the tiny women would soon find out what a *big* man Zhabnov was. Sexually speaking.

The APCs of Zhabnov's soldiers too were all slowly moving away from the final resting place of the Dooms-day Warrior, leaving America's greatest hero behind — forever.

Zhabnov was sure they were clear of the cliff now. Clear of any danger. He clicked the intercom switch on the arm of his command chair and said, "Detonate."

Zhabnov shouted in glee as the explosion shook the cliff behind him, and closed off the entrance to the cavern, sealing his old enemy in eternal darkness. The nuclear generators the little people had built would maintain power for Rockson's metabolic-assist systems. The power would keep him alive — just barely — would keep Rockson in the hell of an endless nightmare!

Zhabnov watched the dust clear, to make sure the tumble of giant stones would completely seal the tomb. It did.

Chapter Nine

Blackness . . . confusion. Then light. Rockson opened his eyes slowly, with difficulty. It felt like they had been glued together. He saw everything through a thick and almost unyielding fog. Not until his mismatched blues were wide open did Rockson realize that he was in some sort of rocket. He had never seen this type of compartment before in his life, but he knew he was in some sort of space craft. And remembered. He remembered being stun-gunned while escaping.

He was in a cubicle that wasn't more than ten by twenty and that was painted white. He was lying on one of several strap-in couches. There were no accessories in sight: no tables, no windows, not even a mirror. Rock felt light, the way you feel when a space ship is in flight. That odd, container-in-motion feeling in his gut wasn't different from what he had experienced during his flight months ago on the trip from Earth to Venus. On that trip, however, there had been a girl whose company he had been able to enjoy, and champagne — paid for by the last money of his failing stock portfolio.

Rock knew that the ship he was riding in wasn't the same as the ship in which he had ridden out to swampy Venus. The passenger lines were more luxurious than this.

The officer had told Rock that he was to be "transported." He must have been put into a spaceship, probably destined for a dismal prison-world. Transported without even the sham of a trial! For *retroactive* crimes!

It was most peculiar that Rock actually found himself looking *forward* to whatever was going to happen next. He didn't resent a fresh experience, as long as he wasn't killed

71

or maimed in the course of it. After all, Venus hadn't been any bargain.

He decided to get to his feet, and found out two other interesting points about his situation. First off, he was strapped down to the couch, which was gravestone shaped. When he tried to loosen the wide nylon belt that tied him in, it soon became apparent that it couldn't be tinkered with. It had a locked snap that could not be unlocked without a key. He could see dark events ahead now. His mouth felt dry as dust.

It put his teeth on edge to be aware that he could have been unconscious for days. He hadn't been at all in control of himself, able to feel what was happening to him, or to know who had been doing what to his body.

What had gone wrong with Kimetta? Why had he suddenly been branded a criminal? It seemed as if reality itself had changed. As if—as if this was a nightmare!

He strained at the straps, looking for an exit from this white-walled prison. No sign of a door was evident. Rock did see a black slash near the ceiling on one of the four walls, but not the accompanying longer slashes from that point to the floor. Could he have been put into a cubicle without any way to get in or out? Panic started rising. Then he controlled his emotions, understanding that he'd better *stay* calm, if he didn't want to start shouting at the top of his lungs. They—whoever they were—might not know he was awake. . . . He almost let out a hard breath, but suddenly stopped himself and clasped his lips tight. He mustn't let them know he was awake.

That was when he heard another's voice.

"Hey, you!" A man's voice, harsh, gritty, as if its owner hadn't spoken for a while. "Which of 'em are you?" the voice asked.

Rock waited, trying to locate the voice.

The voice continued, "I said, which of the prisoners are you?"

He couldn't help asking the unseen man, "Prisoners? What are you talking about?"

72

"Off-world Prison, you damn fool! That's where all of us are being taken!" The voice was surely from another compartment.

Rock had initially supposed that the man talking to him through the wall was one of the jailers. Now he let out a deep breath of relief at knowing that wasn't true. "How many prisoners are there?" Rock asked, desperate for information.

"Five, I think," the gruff voice replied. "One in each of the five strap-chambers."

"Where are we bound?" Rock asked. "What planet?"

"You mean you don't know about it?" A hoarse laugh. "Well, you'd better hold on to your grav-pipe, if you've got one! And it wouldn't hurt you to write a will, either, I tell you that much. We've all been picked for—"

And then the man was still. The words simply stopped coming.

Rock was going to call out, but he heard a smooth hissing nearby and realized that his chamber's wall was opening. A door. It opened from the bottom, toward the slit near the ceiling, like a garage door. He supposed the door had been built in that manner to save space. If he could understand how his captors thought, why they did certain things, it could be useful. He'd pay attention. He'd learn. And escape, somehow.

The sight of the fat policeman who had shot him, now coming into this cubicle, wasn't a surprise, but he did feel a moment's shock at seeing Kimetta behind the shiny-skinned man. He looked down at himself once more as if to make sure that the straps were still on, and then turned his eyes toward Kimetta.

"Why did you turn on me?" She didn't answer. Then he demanded of the jowly man, "What do you mean by tying me down?"

Kimetta glanced at the officer, waiting for him to speak. It occurred to Rock that she couldn't make any motion without being more attractive in his eyes. She wore a scanty, translucent, pale pink sunning suit, stand-

73

ard Venusian beach wear. The kind of clothes that were preferred for a spaceship's constantly warm compartments. Her baby blues were as cute as ever, her strawberry blond hair radiant.

The corporal said, "For once in your life, you'll be of some value to others. We'll see to that!"

Rock asked, "What did I do?" He directed his question to Kimetta. And of course it was the officer who replied, "You've done nothing in your life for anyone else! It's time you did, and perhaps then you will understand! You have been a playboy too long! You will work until—"

He might have added "until you *die*"; those words hung unspoken in the artificial air. Rock glared across at the man. The impassive officer didn't seem either to be enjoying Rock's discomfiture, or to be sorry about it. That aging, shiny, familiar-looking face hadn't been programmed to show emotion.

"You'll be well taken care of," the officer said. His voice was calm and in one key. "During this trip, I mean."

"But not afterwards, I suppose." Rock frowned.

"A number of sanitary robot-tools have been set down near the lower apertures in your body, so that any functions you have to perform can be done. They will perform automatically."

"And I'll be tied up here until the ship lands—is that right?"

"It had been intended for you to be released after the preliminary inspection, and to be permitted to walk around."

Rock looked disdainfully at his plain, ten-by-twenty cubicle.

"Every inch of space is needed," the officer said. "This area, however, is a little larger than strictly necessary."

"Where are we spacing to? You can tell me that much at least!"

"Yes, certainly. We're on our way to Esmerelda. The famous work-asteroid. Kimetta Langdon here made the choice herself."

74

Rock started to say, "I never heard of—," and then realized that Kimetta was going toward the door and that the fat, shiny-skinned man was walking off behind her. He watched the door closing in back of the unlikely couple and shut his eyes briefly. Somewhere else a door was raised and lowered. Then silence. After a while he raised his voice to talk to the harsh-throated man who'd been in communication with him a while ago. "Where's Esmerelda? What is it?"

The unseen man replied at once. "So you don't know 'bout Esmerelda?" *Was the man chuckling?* "You've got a royal treat coming to you!"

"I haven't heard of every rundown little hellhole planet in the galaxy," Rock protested. He'd been too busy going to the best nightclubs, out with the most desirable women. He had filled himself with exotic food and drink and emptied his loins into any number of women he had liked very much at the time and knew he'd never see again. "I haven't been *everyplace*," he added lamely.

"Well, you're never gonna forget Esmerelda, Mac, I tell you that much. It's not a planet at all, not even a small, ugly old planet. It's—*hell!*"

Rock was harsh-voiced himself, now, looking at the wall to his right as if it was the man to whom he spoke. He must be behind a paper-thin partition, to be heard that clearly.

"An asteroid?"

"Right."

"I've heard that humans can live on an asteroid, but how do they manage it? Where does the air come from?"

"Humans can breathe the same way that Esmereldans do. They—*hold on*, somebody's coming! My name's Sanders Bylor," the voice whispered, "and we'll try and look each other up, *if we can, later.*"

The last four words chilled Rock. He was used to being on his own, to going where he wanted. He found himself more alarmed by the minute thinking of an undersized prison planet with a silly name. Why had Kimetta picked it out? *Who* was she?

There was a moment's silence, and then Rock heard a gasp that finished with a sigh. After that, he heard a door close. His own door opened very soon afterwards.

It was Kimetta again. This time, she was by herself. A small, green thumb-tray floated at her side, moving when she raised a finger. He wasn't sure whether the girl herself was floating on air or walking on the floor. Everything he'd heard in the last few minutes had disturbed him, and he wanted to get a little of his own moxie back. He started trying to disconcert the pretty young traitor who stood in front of him.

"You and the slimy officer," he began, "are you lovers?"

She blinked rapidly, but answered the question. "Friends only. You are my love. Or were. Believe me, he's nothing to me."

Rock was mildly surprised at having drawn a not-unfriendly response, which was more than the officer would have handed him.

"Doesn't he *want* to be your lover?"

"Dovine says so," she replied. "But Zhabno Dovine is — asexual. I like him, somewhat. Perhaps because he adores me."

"So you're on a name basis with him! You like him, but not as a lover? You think he's too cold, too distant? That's right?" Rockson was torn by jealousy and confusion. But her little shrug was all the answer Rock needed. It made him feel better, to know that she was not screwing Dovine. Maybe Kimetta could be won over — why not? She had loved him just a few days ago. She could help him escape! If there was enough time on this trip, and there certainly ought to be, then he'd like to become very friendly again with the buxom young woman. No matter what might happen once the ship landed on Esmerelda, wherever that might be, at least he could give Kimetta and himself a good time along the way! Rock was starting to feel that she wouldn't have any more objections than he did. She was smiling warmly at him. Just like the old

76

days.

"It's been decided to make your trip as easy as possible, your's and the others'," she said. "Instead of having to worry and be upset about your duties on Esmerelda, you're to be put *under* for the balance of the day."

"Under?" Rock didn't understand. But it sounded *ominous*.

Kim rapidly undid part of his one-piece, touching the base of his neck with cold thumb and forefinger, pinching the area under his chin.

"What are you doing?"

"Raising the skin, finding a vein," she replied.

She suddenly seemed distracted and instead of reaching for what Rock could now see was the long-needled syringe on the floating tray, she touched a strange blue disk medallion she wore on a chain about her pale neck. "Here, I will put this on you. Wear it forever. Never take it off. It will protect you from the Zrano." She took it off and clasped the medallion around Rock's neck. "My gift to you — in honor of our love."

She smiled mysteriously.

He made a mental note to ask Sanders Bylor what in hell a Zrano might be. All his life as a playboy he had considered himself experienced and able to adapt, but he was going to have a harder time than ever before from now on. He had to have INFORMATION!

"What is a Zrano?"

No answer. Just a wink.

"What is the medallion for?"

"It's a love token," she said, looking down at the medallion. "As long as you wear it, nothing much can happen to you."

Her full lips twitched briefly in a sort of amusement; and Kimetta leaned over him, kissed him; and as he responded with his burning lips Rock felt the sting of a hypodermic needle in his throat!

Chapter Ten

Five hours later he woke up in what he soon realized was another chamber. Rock had awakened in a medium-sized, Earth-style room with a comfortable bed and a bureau with half a dozen buttons to open the slots intended for shoes and one-pieces. There was a new one-piece in one of the open slots, and since he found he wasn't strapped down, he sat up on his cot, took off the stale clothes he was wearing, then washed himself in an adjoining bathroom. He shut the bathroom door before stripping off the smelly suit and putting on the new, blue one-piece. It was the right size. There was a mirror, too. And a comb. Rock was able to comb his long, white-streaked black hair and look at the uncertain cast of his pale features. The sight of that mirror startled him, because he had sometimes seen movies about desperate men, desperate *prisoners,* taking a mirror and breaking it and cutting their wrists with the slivers. He was turning from the mirror when he heard two taps on the door. They were polite, soft, which surprised him.

"Can I come in?" A young man's voice — the wall-man?

"I don't think I could stop you," he replied. "There's no lock."

"Certainly you can, if you want to. Just ask me to come back later." But the door opened a crack. In stared a young man in a red jumpsuit with an emblem of a comet on the lapels.

"Are you one of the guards?"

"I work here, yes," the blond man said apologetically.

"Well, if this is a prison ship, I can't stop you. Come on in. Maybe I'll find out something."

The door was opened all the way. The blond man was a fresh-faced youth, a Venusian whose shiny skin reminded

78

Rockson of Corporal Dovine as he must have been in his youth. He felt a moment's pang at not having seen Kimetta since she put him under, and then winked at the newcomer. "What's the score?" Rock asked. "You have a hypo for me too?"

"Are you comfortable here?" the man asked, looking around. "Everything in order?"

"I don't suppose it's bad, for a prison-ship," Rock admitted.

"You keep using that word. It makes me feel rotten, if you know what I mean."

"I don't see why it should. I'm being sent to Esmerelda. Isn't that true?"

"Obviously," the man smiled, but his eyes were sorrowful.

"What for? Is there a reason?"

"Of course! You are a criminal!"

"What is my sentence? How long?"

"You'll find out very soon now. You're bound to know before we land. I've got to go now."

"Will you answer one more question? You don't have to say yes or no. Maybe I can guess the answer by how you look when I ask — even if you don't tell me. Fair enough?"

The young man turned to leave, unwilling to let Rock see his face give away any response — not everybody on this space craft was as grim and impassive as Dovine, it seemed. Rock realized he could see the man's face in the mirror, and quickly asked: "Has my sentence got anything to do with somebody or something named Zrano?"

He had remembered Kimetta's words about Zrano, and the medallion he wore — her gift — protecting him. But Rock was not absolutely sure that he remembered them *exactly*. The young guard's face showed a furtive discomfort, as if Rock had mentioned something very unpleasant. And then the guard left, saying only, "You'll see! Heaven help you, you'll see!" His hands were at his sides, lips almost prim. "But don't think of tomorrow. There is a treat in store today! If you come out to the hall in an hour, you'll be on the way to a pleasant surprise!"

The compartment door closed in back of him. Rock figured he could have dived after the young man, made it into the corridor, could have held the man as a hostage. *But then what?*

Rock looked in the desk slots for any audi-reads, but found none. Not even a Bible. He went back and stared at his face in the bathroom mirror, then shrugged and looked away. He was used to taking pleasure from others and giving it to them, but not used to plotting. Still, he would escape. Somehow, he would escape.

The outside door didn't open until an hour had drifted past. When it did, there was no one there. He went through the door. He was alone in a long and antiseptically white corridor, facing five closed doors, two others on the same side of the corridor as his room. There wasn't any indication of where to go, or what to do. Right or left? If a long, white corridor could be called confusing, he was certainly confused. His hand went to the circular blue medallion.

A door far down the hall to the right opened halfway. Rock headed in that direction. He half-imagined a pretty girl, maybe Kimetta herself, beckoning with another syringe. He'd not let her put him "under" this time! No way!

Just as he started in that direction, a burly and unshaven man came out of the closer of the other two doors, glanced at him, cocked his head alertly, and then took a step toward Rock.

"I never seen you in my life," the man said, in a harsh voice, the same voice from the wall Rock didn't think he'd ever forget. "You're not from Venus Prison. Who are you?"

"You've spoken to me and I've listened to you," Rock told him calmly. "Don't you recognize my voice?"

"Oh. Oh, yeah. You're in the next cube! Well, lots of luck, sonny." The man squinted again. "You're no older than 'bout forty, I'd guess. Did you have a nice life?"

Rock said, "More or less." Funny, he wasn't at all sure how old he was! Effect of the drug?

"Things like this, they hadn't ought to happen to guys like me who never had a break, shoved from prison world to prison world. Unlucky, that's me. I, who haven't been around, haven't seen much."

Rock wasn't going to comment about that. "What's going to happen to us?" he asked instead.

The burly man seemed distracted. "As I said, my name's Sanders Bylor." He shoved forward a ham hock hand. "Pleased to meet you."

"Rock's my name. Niles Rockson."

He took the huge hand. To his astonishment, something seemed to tickle his palm and he realized that the handshake was a ruse. Something had been put into his hand! Rockson drew his hand back and looked down at it. A gray audi-writing square! A message!

Sanders Bylor made an urgent gesture toward a flap of the new one-piece that Rock was wearing. He put the audi-writing square away, supposing that Sanders, as a long-time prisoner, was used to living with small intrigues. Everything he did that authority wouldn't know about was a triumph perhaps; a small but solid triumph . . .

Rock looked down the corridor at the door that had opened. Nothing. No one had come out there.

He couldn't help asking, "What were you arrested for?"

"Smuggling, if that makes any difference now. How I figured to get away with a smuggling job on Venus I'll never know. The way it is, kid, is that you hear stories about other people who did things, and you suppose you can do 'em. So you smuggle slumph-crystals from the Alpha Centauri quadrant and you get caught and you get put in the cruncher. That's all there is to it. After that — it's up to them. Your life isn't your own anymore. What are you in for?"

"I don't know. I think for being a playboy. Didn't know it was illegal!"

"Oh yeah! Retroactive laws are a bummer aren't they," the man said.

"What's going to happen to us on Esmerelda?" Rock

81

asked, coming back to the subject of greatest interest to both of them.

"Kid, I'm not exactly sure. If it was some ordinary prison planet we'd been taken to, I'd say it was a so-called medical experiment with us prisoners to be used as material. On Esmerelda, I doubt it. From what I've heard, they're pretty much a no-nonsense group there. Into the work ethic. Period. And lots of rules. Anything that gets done around there, kid, there's a rule. Know what I mean?"

Rock nodded, though he didn't, and asked, "Do you think it's got anything to do with somebody named Zrano? Our being brought to Esmerelda in the first place, I mean."

Sanders Bylor's reaction wasn't measured, like the guard's. The burly man pulled back as if Rock had developed some contagious disease. His eyes widened in horror and he drew up one large hand as if to fend off an attack.

"Oh my *God,* no," he whispered. "They can't do that to you! They can't do that to me! Not just for being a smuggler! Heaven help us kid. I'll pray for you and me, I swear!"

A bell rang. Another door opened. A voice could be heard over a public address system. "This is the captain. If you haven't opened your door yet, you can now open it." It was a sexless voice without feeling, a voice that could have belonged to a machine. "You must walk to the right end of the corridor, the end with a purple light over the exit door. You then walk through that door and to the next door and open it."

Men came out of each door. Six men in all, counting Rock. The men looked awkwardly at each other, nodded. "All in the same boat," their expressions stated glumly. Sanders broke the silence by smiling. He walked toward the purple sign. They drew apart to give him room. "Don't any of you men want to have something good happen?" Sanders asked. "Come on! Let's have fun!"

Rock followed. They all filed into a long hallway that

82

wasn't as well lighted, but was more comfortable to the eyes than the harsh light of their corridor. He could hear murmurs and grunts back of him, and realized that the remaining prisoners were walking more slowly, discussing something under their breaths.

Rock and Sanders came to another slide-up door. Sanders put a thumb just above the door lock and it drew up. Rock's mouth opened in astonishment at what the slowly opening door revealed: a set up for a party. Balloons on the ceiling, red and blue. A bunting-decorated banquet room containing a long table with three chairs on each side. On a dais was another table, this one with three chairs. In front of each place setting at the lower table was a dish with food that fairly steamed, and enticing smells rose in waves of seductive warmth.

Food! When was the last time he ate! Rock hadn't eaten a good meal since before he slept with Kimetta on Venus; this was like finding gold in a tar pit. The other prisoners behind him let out deep breaths.

"You think they'd bring us this far so they could poison us?" one skinny prisoner asked suspiciously. "This looks too good!"

And then came Sanders Bylor's harsh voice: "No, it'll be a whole lot worse than that, guys, when they get around to finishing us off. This is the *good* part, to make the *bad* part that much worse!"

Rock was already on his way to a place setting to the right. He forked up some meat. At his taste of the first mouthful, he smiled. "Pot roast — or synth-roast at least! I think I'm going to enjoy being on this prison ship for a while." Of course, he said that because he suspected They listened.

Chapter Eleven

The meal wasn't like any that Rock had ever eaten. Only the sight of the empty chairs at the table on the dais kept him from enjoying completely a meal that was made up of clams a la Mars Canal, chicken con Jupiter with garnish Ursa Majors, and octagonal-shaped meat-bun pastries a la Orion. Over his synth-coffee, Rock looked around at the others. They had finished, and were leaning back well satisfied.

"At least we've all got a good meal under our belts," Rock said, eyeing the men, gauging them.

"*You* have," the skinny, pock-faced prisoner growled. "I never seen anybody eat the way you do, kid, like every bite was heaven on a plate."

Another prisoner said, "You probably haven't got stomach trouble, like the rest of us. The stuff they give you in Venus Prison could kill a space pilot!"

Rock remarked, "I've eaten all of these fine dishes before, not too long ago, and they all tasted half as good."

"A dinner like this at Jupiter Work Release Detention Center I could believe," one of the older men remarked. He was shaking his head slowly. "On a prison ship—well, a dinner like this has *got to* be paid for in some way. And in heavy credits, too, if you ask me."

Sanders said grimly, "I'd feel a little better if we'd had bread and water instead of being fattened up."

Rock thought they were being too suspicious.

There was a sudden attention-getting cough from the direction of the dais. Corporal Dovine stood behind a table, his shiny skin reflecting the ceiling light. Two attractive girls in modest blue dresses were seating themselves in the other chairs. They folded their hands demurely before them, and modestly cast down their blue eyes. Neither was as pretty as Kimetta and Rock lost interest in them for the moment. A sharp intake of breath could be heard from the other men at this table though, and Rockson realized that they probably hadn't been this close to any women in a long, *long* while.

Dovine said, "I'm going to assume that all of you are resentful at having been brought forcibly aboard. I ask you to remember a few facts about our destination before you go overboard in detesting it and those of us who live there. No doubt you're all aware that life on an asteroid is always hard, that asteroids have been settled only because of overpopulation on larger planets. I wonder if you understand many of the problems involved in creating a livable space on an asteroid. I trust that the good meal you have been given will dispose you to thinking about this."

He paused to look at each prisoner. His eyes might have narrowed when they reached Rock, but it was impossible to be sure. Probably a man such as Dovine would have preferred to die before showing his true feelings. His personality would have suited a hermit-stoic, but his work was always putting him in front of people. Had anybody ever laughed with Dovine? Touched the man? What makes a man like that?

"For example, there is no atmosphere on Esmerelda, as that word is generally understood. The air you will breathe is," Dovine went on, "entirely artificial. There is no true sun, no moons. In order to survive with the benefits of technology all of you who will live on the asteroid must take pills that have the side effects of making your skin gleam as mine does. I have been told that the result—cosmetically—is considered bad by many of those on Earth and Venus, and even by some spacers."

Rockson heard a muttered remark from Sanders but couldn't make out the words. If Dovine heard anything, he gave no sign. He continued, "Life on this asteroid revolves itself into patterns of hard work." Dovine continued, "I too will live there most of this year—and work hard. Even such amusements as we have aboard this ship are absent there. I think you can understand, those of you who have been imprisoned elsewhere, that amusements on this planetoid, because they are hard to come by, thus are cherished. Those who provide the scant entertainment are highly regarded."

He stopped long enough to drink from a yellow cup emblazoned with twin comets. Perhaps it was strong alcohol, for he gasped a little before he continued.

"In *your* cases, all of you—and I assume that you would rather hear about yourselves—are to be sent there to work hard, as do all the many fine natives of this asteroid. If you succeed, honor and glory and a lifetime of freedom without want will be waiting for you."

He paused, allowing time for somebody to ask what would happen if the prisoners failed. No one spoke. The answer was clear. All the same, Dovine, being the man he was, had to make the point clearly:

"If you *fail,* none of those desirable consequences will be yours. Not one, not even a longer lifetime. It will be *over* for your miserable lives. I hope I've made myself understood! You'll have a chance, a perfectly fair chance to obtain what you want. But you must work for it."

Sanders made a soft hissing sound between his teeth, more of a reflex than a comment.

"There seems to be a certain dissatisfaction among you," Dovine said, and Rock would have sworn that he was dryly amused. "I'll accept questions."

The prisoner at Rock's left, a mournful-looking, fiftyish man with very few teeth, asked, "What work have we got to do?"

"I'm afraid it will take a day or two once we land before we can sort that out," Dovine said. "For reasons beyond my control entirely. In the meantime, you are the guests of our spacecraft. Eat well, sleep well. I regret that there is no work for you on this short journey, but that condition will soon pass, believe me."

Somebody snickered. It was the horse-faced prisoner who'd made a remark about such a good dinner having to be paid for.

"I've done 'nough work in my time. A little relaxation is what I need," Horse-face said.

An emotion flickered behind Dovine's eyes, and Rock could guess what it was. Sadism. The eager anticipation of seeing that man in agony. But nobody could deny that Dovine was a master of self-control. His response was mild and measured. "A few days of total leisure will make Esmerelda much more . . . interesting," Dovine said mildly. "Are there any other questions?"

"Yes." Rock stood up and turned to face the man directly for the first time since coming into this ritzy banquet room. "Is there a Mr. Zrano involved in this? And when are we supposed to meet him?"

Dovine's lips pursed tightly a long time before he spoke. "I must give a truthful answer to each part of that question. No, there isn't a Mr. Zrano involved. However, you will meet Zrano in the course of your — involvement in the entertainments. If the warden-president of Esmerelda decides that."

Rockson didn't like the sound of that. This Zrano seemed to be a *thing*, not a man! Rock absentmindedly touched the moon-shaped medallion hung around his neck. Protection against *Zrano* . . .

"All right, then," Rock complained, "animal, vegetable, or mineral — is Zrano something that's *not* human, and that we're all going to be involved with?"

"The answer to both questions is in the affirmative," Dovine said, and Sanders let out a deep despairing breath. "I think that will be all for the questions," Dovine snapped. "Everything you want to know is going to be answered shortly, perhaps sooner than you might wish. Are there requests that haven't been anticipated? Is there anything you want that you can realistically be given now and in the terms of your short stay here?"

The question had been framed to rule out bad jokes of

the sort that inspired requests for freedom or for passage back to Venus. Dovine may not have had any humor himself, but he'd probably heard that others did.

Rock said promptly, "I want the company of a woman."

Everyone at the prisoners table except Sanders chuckled and nodded.

"Me, too."

"Same here."

"Yeah, a blond with curves."

Surprisingly, Dovine replied, "Women will be provided, but only for brief spans of time. I regret that, but any consort has to earn her credits. You have only a small number of credits each — the pay you have coming for good behavior. So be *good*. And — we'll see."

Rock was a bit amazed. Women were to be *provided?*

"If all of you will return to your rooms, women will soon be with those of you who ask for them. These two women here are available for thirty credits per hour. You don't get to choose which one." Dovine pushed back his chair, took another drink, then said, "Thank you for having listened to me so courteously."

Rock thought that the man's eyes lighted briefly on Sanders, and then Dovine walked off the dais and out a suddenly opening door. The two women who'd sat with him so passively now got to their feet and followed, after a momentary pause. The room was quiet once more. All eyes had followed the women.

Rock and the others were advised over the P.A. to hurry back toward the rooms they'd been given. No dessert.

"Hey, you!" It was Sanders. The burly man touched Rock's shoulder with a hard hand as they filed out of the room.

"What do you want?"

Sanders, not saying another word, only pointed at the flap in Rock's one-piece that had received the gray square of audi-writing a while ago.

88

Rock nodded. He walked on, into his room, noticing that his wall mirror had been taken away in the half-hour's absence. With the gray square firmly in hand, he flipped the toggle at the bottom and heard Sanders's first words spoken so quietly that the speak-end had to be raised to his ear to hear: "There ain't no more room for *workers* on Esmerelda, I hear. Once we land, pal, we have to get away before the Zrano gets us." Sanders's desperate urgency was entirely convincing, but it was unfortunate that he took it for granted that Rock knew what a Zrano might be. "Anything's better than *that*," Sanders whispered from the device, "I've heard stories from men who wouldn't lie to me. There are—deserted places—badlands on that asteroid where a man can hide. Now in order to get away, we've—"

A knock at the door. Rock clicked off the device.

Not for a moment was Rock seriously tempted to hear Sanders's words out to the end, not just *then*. He didn't seriously believe that it would be possible to get away once they'd landed, so it seemed that Sanders's sputtering could wait for awhile. He tucked the audi-writing away in the flap from which he had drawn it. Rock said, "Come in." He smiled at the girl who walked in, even though she wasn't Kimetta.

"My name is Qettm," she said briskly. "Let us begin."

She was the one who had sat at Dovine's right side. A good-looking girl by any standards, she wore an attractive, green, low-cut mini-outfit. Barefooted, she probably was a little taller than his five-eleven, which Rock didn't mind at all. She could have been any age from twenty to thirty-five—the shiny skin made it hard to tell with any certainty. She flopped on the cot, as if she wanted to be finished with the "work" ahead as fast as possible, and started to unbutton her outfit.

He was still trying to pronounce her name when she peeled off her scanties, looking at him expectantly, suddenly utterly naked. She was ripe. Probably a lot of synth-buildup, but a good job. He got into bed. The girl said, "Do what is normal and necessary."

Rock wasn't like that. He insisted on being slow, making diversions, touching her in this place and that, prolonging the ritual so as to please *her* as well as himself. He knew he was slowly bringing her close to the heights of ecstasy. She responded, and they began doing what they *both* now desperately wanted to do!

When it was over, Qettm said warmly, "There is no charge, and I want to stay, so that you can do *that* another hundred times! But I have to go. I'll come back soon!"

"I'd like that," Rock said. "When?"

"I will return, if possible, in an hour."

Now, they were friends. Her cold gray eyes had changed, and become a warm pair of baby blues. "Never was a man so kind to a girl," she spoke, as she slipped on her scanties. "I never had any pleasure from the sex act."

"I can't believe that," Rock said, finding a cigarette.

"On Esmerelda, sex is performed because children have to be made or because some people find the pressure of not doing it for a while to be intolerable." Qettm raised herself up reluctantly. "Only so much time allotted for sex during a month, and after that you have to get out and do your work. It is the system, for citizens as well as prisoners. It is, they say, for our own good."

Rockson nodded. All tyranny, he knew, sought to control joy, to deny the "feeling" part of life. *For your own good,* the rulers of Esmerelda said, *for your own effectiveness, you have to be deprived of joy.*

"With you," Qettm added lowly, "I wish sex to last for many months! There's no one like you on all of Esmerelda. Something about being with you is different from other men I've known."

He couldn't bring himself to say that the difference was simply that he enjoyed making *her* happy, and as a result she had set herself to make him very happy in turn. There was probably an Esmereldan dictionary

90

with a definition of the word "pleasure," but any citizen stumbling across it probably raised his eyebrows and hurried away to find another more comfortable word. He felt a pang of empathy for her.

After Qettm put on her clothes, she turned on impulse to kiss Rock full and warmly on the lips.

"There! I never did that before unless I knew I was going to make extra credits with the man! I must thank you for having caused me to feel so good, for giving me — *hope?* Is that the word? Yes, hope that there is more than work."

Not until she was gone, having used her voice-activation code to get out of the room, did Rock lazily remind himself that he ought to have asked about the Zrano. The audi-writing was still available to him, of course.

Sanders's clear and urgent tones came through at his touch, as he lay puffing on a Camel: "I've heard stories from men who wouldn't lie to me. Now in order to get away we have to meet in the main square, called The Concourse, as soon as possible. The first one out on the asteroid will try to get all the others to join the escape. Six have a better chance of making it. There won't be any trouble putting the guards out of commission. All it needs is a few sharp-edged metallic objects and a little guts. From the minute we get back to our rooms where they take us, we've got to get busy. Hide something sharp in your one-piece! Remember, our lives depend on it. Remember, it's escape, or the Zrano!"

Rock turned it off and crushed out his cig. Escape? There was no sense trying to get away from an asteroid if there was no ship waiting to fly you away. Rock wondered if Sanders was sane. He tilted the audi-writing square so that the long, thin sliver of toggle would fall out. He watched it dissolve. Once the evidence was self-destroyed, Rockson put his considerable skill in mimicking voices to use. He imitated the sex-girl's voice and after three tries, the door slid open, activated by his close copy of her throaty tones. He had decided to talk

Sanders and the others out of doing themselves harm by making any escape try. The penalty for attempted escaping, everyone knew, was *brain-sapping* — a ray that basically erases your mind. That wouldn't do! The others might disagree, but he'd talk about making the best of this situation. Maybe Rock had found his true vocation at last: "Realist!" Or "Model prisoner!"

Nobody was in this narrow white corridor. Were there guards in this area? Cameras? Stun-traps?

Sanders's door was wide open. Had he figured out how to open it also?

Rock guessed what he would find inside Sanders's room. And sure enough, the room was empty, all right. It was as if Sanders hadn't ever been there. Maybe the man was roaming around looking for booze? Or was already trying an escape — in space! If so, it seemed like a stupid gesture to have left the door open. Rock wondered why he suddenly felt as if he had sustained a bad chill.

"Going somewhere?" It was Dovine's voice, which startled him.

Rock spun around. "I—"

"It's all right," Dovine smiled, "you were very clever to get out of your room. Now you wonder what happened to Sanders? Well, he was a *bad* boy. He was plotting you know. We had to let him take a stroll . . ."

"Stroll?"

"Yes," Dovine smirked, coming closer, slapping a swagger stick in his hands. "Sanders has taken a walk outside the spacecraft. Without a spacesuit. He won't be back."

Chapter Twelve

Fourteen hours later, after a sleep period:

"Step inside, please," Dovine said. "I hope that the last one will close the door." There were only five of them now: Rock, Skinny Jones, Reelk, Jansen and Horse-face.

Reelk, the mournful-looking prisoner with only a few teeth, was the last in, and did what he had been asked. Rockson noticed with relief that all four other prisoners had come in response to the order to report to Dovine. So Sanders was the *only* one jettisoned. The dining table had been taken away, and five chairs faced the dais now. Two dull gray boxes had been set down on the table in front of Dovine, one at each end.

"You all will be seated. There will be no need to discuss Sanders at this meeting—is that clear?"

No one said anything.

Rock was the only prisoner to sit down so that the bright ceiling light wouldn't batter down on his head.

"You've *killed* him," Reelk blurted. And then he held a fist against his blabbermouth.

"No," Dovine replied. "He had a fair chance to survive," Dovine spoke smoothly. "Not as fair as some of you will get, but as much chance as he deserved. He tried to escape in a shuttle capsule and he hadn't properly sealed its air lock. So, I didn't do anything, not really. Just let him—escape."

"I don't believe you," Rock said. "You killed him."

Dovine just shrugged. "I'm innocent."

"You've got no right to kill Sanders," the toothless one continued to mutter.

"Please be *quiet* and watch." Dovine moved a switch

on the box to his right and another on the one to his left. The boxes were visi-screens, it seemed, for they soon presented identical pictures. The video pictures were of a gladiator-type arena. It was empty. Rock felt his muscles knot up at the sight; he had the feeling he didn't want to see this tape.

"What in the name of hell is going on?" Reelk muttered as they waited for the action. "What is this stuff?"

"We're probably going to watch visi-flicks, like a bunch of damn kids," Jansen, the fat one, complained.

"At least it's something to do," the lantern-jawed Horse-face said, fidgeting. "I didn't get a prosti-visit. I had no good behavior credits and—I've been biting my nails down to the armpits without anything in the way of work."

"Shut up!" Dovine snapped. "Just look!" On the screen, the camera panned up, showing an expectant audience of about five hundred people in the arena, maybe more. Rock wondered who the guy with a whole box to himself was. He was old, looked mean, and was dressed sort of like Nero would have been, laurel wreath and all.

"That's the warden on the goddamn prison-asteroid," Reelk said. "He used to be warden on Venus. His name is Langdon."

"Hey, look now! There's the bottom of the arena! That's where it's all gonna happen, whatever *it* is," Jansen shouted.

"It's gonna be like one of those shows you see on Venus-Blue where two guys beat each other's brains out," Reelk offered.

Rockson wished they would shut the hell up. But Skinny Jones said, "No, it's not! Look at those gates, one very big, and one about human size. Reminds me more of an arena for those Spanish bullfights! But that gate is way too big for any bull I ever heard of."

Something dark was coming out of that large gate.

"That's no bull. It's only got two legs," Reelk said, in

a low tone. "God, what is it?"

The *thing*, a massive black shape, stayed in shadows. Out of the small gate came a man—a naked, well-muscled man. He was being prodded out with long pointed tridents by two uniformed guards. The guards were laughing; the naked man was crying.

Reelk said, "Jeez! He's turning back to the little gate, like he'd give anything to be back on the other side."

"Poor bastard!" Rock muttered. Having guessed what was going to happen, Rockson watched Dovine's expressionless face, the face of somebody very, very evil. Horse-face said, "Look at that other gate! The big one! Something's coming now. Whatever it is, it's huge!"

"It's coming, now," Reelk agreed.

Rock saw a dark, immense shape moving in the shadows, and then nothing! The camera panned down, and avoided giving a clear shot of the thing! Frustrating!

For a split second, Rock thought they had seen something like an elephant-sized lizard-creature, something out of every man's nightmares, a four-o'clock-in-the-morning creature, a hangover creature. But he wasn't sure.

The camera had moved so quickly that Rock couldn't be sure it wasn't just his mind filling in a *shape*. The camera *did* show the naked victim, with his back against the sharp, guard-held pikes that had propelled him into the arena. He was letting go of his bowels, and screaming. To show a human being who looked the way that man did at that moment was in itself a wicked act. *Not* seeing the thing made it worse.

In a low, awed voice one of the prisoners asked, "What *is* it? I didn't see."

"Well," Dovine said, "I guess it's a Zrano."

Rockson didn't have to look up at Dovine to know that the man would be smiling.

Horse-face said quietly, "The guy has got no place to

run, it ain't fair."

"Hell, if it was me out there, I'd run like nobody's business!" Reelk said with conviction.

"You?" Horse-face looked cynically at the speaker. "You'd probably *shit* that damn thing to death!"

Rock wondered if it wasn't the ability to make bad jokes in times of stress that set human beings apart from other species. His eyes were riveted on the screen and, like the other prisoners in the room, he couldn't help talking; but his words were aimed at Dovine.

"Why is this being done?"

"You should understand that, of all people. It is a punishment. A simple pleasure for the audience, a punishment for the victim."

"Is the sight of a man's dying horribly your idea of —"

"The people of Esmerelda, you realize, work very hard indeed. It shouldn't surprise you if they want to watch others suffer a bit too? This is a live broadcast, by the way. Many prisoners on Esmerelda have *volunteered* to face the Zrano. They think it's better than living there."

"Has anybody ever survived?" Reelk asked — a good question.

"Oh yes, indeed. There's a gentleman who died very recently of old age who had met the mother of this Zrano. Zranos are living fossils. Monsters very rare indeed, worth *quite* a lot of credits. I might tell you, if it's of interest, that there will be no descendants of this monster, alas. The rules of biology are immutable, and the birth of this Zrano resulted in — ah, difficulties. At any rate, the games will never resume unless it is with a Zrano-robot, once this one dies. I'm sure a robot-monster won't be as good."

This "game" would be over quickly, Rock thought. The monster, its form obscured by a blur deliberately placed in the transmission, located the victim's quaking form and was moving toward him. It lumbered, but its size was enough to cut off the only possible avenue of retreat, the still-open large gate. The victim's eyes were half-closed, face twisted in pain now. His lips narrowed primly. His right hand left his face and drifted up into a raised position. "We who are about to die salute you, warden," he said. Rockson was surprised at that.

The camera zoomed in briefly on the audience, on the mean-looking bastard with a whole box to himself. He yawned, apparently not even interested in what was happening. He was bending over and talking to somebody in the box below: a woman, who fanned herself and tittered. They were joking.

"Now! Here it comes!" Jansen shouted.

The shape, distorted deliberately again by a device in the camera lens, had cornered the man, and the burly victim screamed out and pulled a dagger. He suddenly charged, a last show of courage! The Zrano raised what would have been a paw in any other monster; it was blurry. *Maybe* it was a claw, like a lobster claw, Rock suspected.

The view on the visi-screen cut suddenly to the carpet of greenery below the victim's feet. There was a spurt of dark liquid on it, and another . . . bloodcurdling screams with each splash. Now the camera showed the audience on its feet, all cheering. The camera panned back to the scene of "battle." Now the blurred-out monster was obviously stepping on what was left of a human, doing a three-legged waltz on it. The man's head vanished under one of the huge clawed feet. Rock didn't look away. If he was to face this thing, any information he could gather could mean something, could give him a slim chance. . . . Damn! It was worse, not seeing it, seeing just the blur.

He was aware of Dovine standing and flicking the pair of viewers off simultaneously. The pictures seemed to fold in on themselves.

All the men were looking awkwardly in Dovine's direction, waiting for him to speak. Rock finally asked, "When do we go up against—it?" His words came slowly, carefully even in tone. The other prisoners were shocked.

"The games are held every month, except for a special meeting like the one you just saw," Dovine intoned. "Special meetings happen very rarely—only on holidays. Today is Planetoid Day, so we were lucky, weren't we?"

"How much time do we have?"

"You all will face the Zrano Tuesday, the next scheduled meeting."

"In four days." It was Horse-face now, his voice rising. "But we *can't* possibly learn to beat a monster in such a short time! We want to work! Please, I'll be good!"

"You will have as good a chance against the Zrano as anybody, prisoner. More than that, no one on Esmerelda could offer you. You'll be armed. Armaments are chosen by lot; some are better than others!"

"It's not enough," the mournful-looking Reelk said. "You're sending all of us out there to die."

But Dovine had turned and was already on his way out of the banquet hall.

"I w-want to WORK, not die," Horse-face whimpered to no one in particular. "Why did he say before we were going there to *work?* Why?"

Rockson answered with one word: "Sadism."

Chapter Thirteen

A day later—a day in which Rockson was confined to quarters and had no visitors—they landed on Esmerelda. He saw nothing of the approach to the asteroid, just felt the ship change direction, and the bump of the landing.

The prisoners were led into an airlock compartment and then off-loaded directly into a jet car. They sat where they were told while a computer set the course. The jet car took them from the landing site past gray fields and rickety-looking cubical houses toward a looming arena. The one they had seen on the visi-screen, no doubt. The planetoid looked like a vast city.

The colors of the cubelike buildings were bright pink and gold. When they stopped and filed inside one cube-building's lobby, Rock saw that the inside was a series of natural pastel shades, with a carpet of artificial grass. Rock had formed a different impression from the visi-screen pictures, expecting some grim exteriors, dark interiors; but this place looked cheerful and was well kept. People strolled by, smiling, looking happy, well fed. Many were couples. Several guards with max-stun guns watched them.

The imitation air made him cough. It smelled like excrement. The sky, seen through an oculum, was lighted with a small yellow sun—artificial for sure. His coughing fit didn't stop until Rock was separated from the others and led into a sealed room. Two men came after a while out of a doorway, and faced him. One snapped a bracelet on Rockson.

The leaden-eyed man said, "Unlike the last man to die, you will be able to train against the Zrano. You have a chance. Now, come to the arena. Disobey, and that pain-bracelet is activated."

Rock, as he followed, wondered if the "obedience bracelet" around his right wrist was infallible. Maybe the pain that was transmitted to it if he disobeyed was endurable. He deviated slightly from the suggested path and a white-hot, agonizing pain shot up from the bracelet. One guard smiled. "That's a no-no." Rock returned to the straight-and-narrow and found his eyes moving toward the wide gate ahead, which turned out to be the northeast gate of the stadium — it connected directly to this building.

His coughing fit resumed. The air here was worse. One of the guards suddenly blocked his way. "Stop! Why do you cough? Haven't you been given tiblets?"

"Given what?"

"Every Esmerelda native takes 'tiblets' to prolong life in this artificial air environment," the blond man said.

"Is that the stuff that makes everybody's skin look as if it had been shined?" Rock snapped. "No thanks."

"It prolongs life." The guard's shrug dismissed an irrelevancy, "and the smell goes away. At least you can't smell it. I mean the air *seems* to get better. We'll get you some."

Rock looked sullenly toward the man, and shrugged.

The guard, a fresh edge in his voice, asked, "You're Rockson, aren't you? Niles Rockson, famous playboy? Follow me, I'll fix you up."

Rock again shrugged. "Do I have a choice?" He walked behind the guard and over to the lowest circle of hard blue spectator seats. They had come right out into the stadium proper.

The guard said brusquely, "Sit down here, I'll get you some tiblets." He went away. Rock just coughed and stared out at the porters washing the red off the floor in the far end of the arena with mops and detergent. Shortly, the blond guard returned with a glass of water and two pills. "Swallow these. They last twenty-four hours. You'll be fine."

"Yeah," Rock said swallowing the pills, "sure."

Some men were being led into the arena below the seats now. They were the prisoners from the ship. They all were dressed in gladiator gear; some had nets, some swords. They began to "practice," fighting a laughable wooden replica of a Zrano that was rolled out for them to hit.

"They are being instructed about what to do against the Zrano," the blond guard said. "It's not for you."

"Why can't I be with them?" Rock asked.

"You don't know? I suppose you don't know why you were made the subject of a special game?"

"I can guess — the severe nature of my crime? Play-boyism?"

"Yes, but more than that, dust from a destroyed audi-writing tablet was found during a search of your room. You were actively plotting with Sanders — part of a conspiracy to escape."

"I see."

The guard shrugged. "You do the crime, you pay in a short time." He smiled. "It rhymes, you see?"

"And I suppose I'm going to be punished by having *less* of a chance against the Zrano? What will *my* weapon be?"

"You'll have more of a chance than your friends." The guard was brusque now. "Come on. We'll go join them. You can listen to what the others are told, but you can take no part in the physical exercises they go through. Orders."

Chapter Fourteen

The "trainer" was a huge, leather-outfitted man whose long red hair was combed almost like an ocean wave. He stood with both feet apart as he spoke to the prisoner-trainees.

"You're going to run around the surface of this arena to develop your familiarity with the total area. That'll be helpful to keep you from getting overly excited when the Zrano is facing you. We will run first, and then walk and then run. Now follow me! Everyone except Rockson here."

The exercises, such as they were, Rock noticed, posed no problems for most of the prisoners, but Skinny Jones was sweating furiously before they had moved halfway down the length of the arena. Rock was aware of an occasional envious glance in his direction from the men in the wide pit, because he didn't have to do anything except listen. It *did* strike him as ironical. He always had it easier, didn't he? He wondered about Kimetta. What was she doing? He touched the blue medallion pendant on his chest. They had let him keep it, laughing when he said it would protect him. Would it?

When an hour had passed in walking and running, the burly trainer ordered, "Sit down now men, and I'll be able to give you some good news."

The men flopped down next to Rockson on the well-barbered grass, but the skinny prisoner lay down flat, breathing hard.

"Now I'm going to tell you what I'll spend the balance of the week repeating, so as to din it into your ears in hopes of understanding coming to you all. The Zrano can be beaten, it can be cheated of its prey. A man who is both smart *and* quick can do it. That fact makes the encounter a sporting event, you see, and keeps the people of Esmerelda both alert and interested. It is possible for this reason: the Zrano has strength and size, as you well have seen, but not true intelligence. It is the human beings who have that. You must bear that fact in mind, and use your innate common sense."

Almost breathless, the skinny prisoner spoke bitterly, "What good is brains against something like *that?*"

"The purpose of the contest is to find out," the trainer smiled, "and give the citizens a thrill at the same time."

"Give us some help," Jansen pleaded. "Tell us its weak points."

"To get down and discuss actual cases, I understand that in the year 2096, a man put one arm into the previous Zrano's mouth, cracking a number of its teeth. The beast wrenched that man's arm out of its socket, but was so angry afterwards that it lay down in the middle of the arena and wouldn't continue with the game. Zranos have *pride.*"

"A shrewd cookie, all right," the mournful one said sardonically. "Fellow who lost his arm, I mean. Did he—"

"Yes, he lived. And well! For the human player, as I have pointed out, the objective of this game is to survive. Period. Survive and the world is your oyster."

Rock found himself nodding at that. He *would* survive. He didn't depend on the medallion, but he had *always* been clever. There had to be something *simple* he could do to defeat the Zrano and keep his arm too!

"The arm trick won't work anymore. That Zrano was old," the trainer said. "As to the how of your survival, that's up to you. A man who died not long ago of old age managed to kick the old Zrano so severely that the beast was unable to retaliate for a long time. The game was declared finished by excessive overtime and so he won. Let me point out that you only need to survive for twenty minutes. As for *that* second player, the one I just spoke of, he had trained on Earth as a dancer. He was extremely agile. You can do *anything* to defeat the monster; you have all the latitude in the world. Dirty tricks are fair play."

"That's going to be a big help," the skinny man pointed out. Nobody laughed.

Rock, listening intently, nodded again to himself. *Dirty tricks!* That was the way. It always was.

Rockson was given a small, clean single room in the upper area of the arena. He had a nice soft bed and he fell asleep at once when the light was shut off.

But he dreamed. No, it wasn't a dream. It was a nightmare. Someone might have asked "What could be worse than his *real* life?" The dream was. In the dream, he was sealed in something called a "nightmare coffin." The air in there was bad, he was dreaming bad dreams. He was sealed inside a coffin, inside a cavern. Alone. Buried alive. Alone. Dreaming . . . dreaming he was about to face a thing called a Zrano.

With a start he sat bolt upright, covered with sweat. He was gasping. He took two of the air-purifying "tiblets."

A routine was worked out for them during the next few days, which was comforting somehow. Rockson and the other prisoners would wake up, join together for eats and drinks, then go down to the arena floor. The others would train and Rock would read (or watch). Then they *all* would see visi-screen films of previous meets with the blurry monster, eat again, and spend the balance of each night in their rooms—God knows the others complained they had nothing to do there, but Rock was given a pile of books he requested.

Rock started pumping the blond guard for information on why he wasn't required to train, and why he was given nice quarters and books. The guard said rumor had it a woman named Kimetta Langdon, who was well placed in the hierarchy, being the warden's daughter, had arranged it. Rock slept better for *that* thought. The traitoress might be changing her stripes again. Maybe he had a chance after all. But—how come Kimetta had never told him about her father's job?

Rock spotted a window slit high in the arena so he knew when it was day and night outside; and the exact stages in between could be observed by anybody who could catch a glimpse of the guards' impressive gold wristwatches. Really, though, the day was a matter of artificial lighting, and darkness followed on exact schedule. Rock found himself in a state of rising edginess that didn't involve thinking of the Zrano at all. In one way *only* could it be alleviated, he decided. He wanted to make love to a woman.

At the third day's supper, he asked the blond guard if he could send a girl to his room. Preferably an "A-1" girl called Qettm. The guard arranged for a visit, but it was, sadly, a different "A-1" girl. Nevertheless, Rock made love happily to her and to the different girls he was sent every evening. He was astonished at the proficiency of the women. They were all green-heads, fiery Esmereldan green-heads.

The first one, whose name was Pattok, told him warmly, "I've never been with anybody like you before."

The second, Jeami, remarked, "I didn't know sex could make me feel so good."

The third girl's, Kamoo's, testimonial was just as enthusiastic. "Everything that the other girls say about you is the Esmereldan truth." Rockson was making lots of female allies!

The fourth night's visitor showed her gratitude in another way, pleasing both of them additionally in a manner that Rock, for all his playboy experience, had never encountered: the "Esmereldan position." It would be difficult to explain.

Chapter Fifteen

By the second week of nontraining, Rock was calm and relatively at ease. Reelk, the toothless prisoner with the mournful expression, had ventured to take on a Callistan steak at supper one night, while the pudgy Jansen was stoking himself with two different meats and a regimen of Esmereldan sprouts and vegetables. The food was extra good this night, and *that* made Rock suspect the worst. The training was over. None of the life-preserving tiblets were offered to the prisoners this night — most likely because they weren't expected to survive their all-too-soon-encounter with the Zrano. There wasn't any point wasting any air-pills on them. Rock was eating lightly. If he was right, he'd need to be *fast*.

Jansen noted Rock's slackness at eating and figured out its meaning. He put down his fork. "This is it, right Mr. Rockson, isn't it?" he whispered to Rock.

"Just a guess," Rockson whispered back.

Reelk said, "You'll be sorry now you weren't toughened up by training. I've heard that you've had a different girl every night — it weakens one, you know! You'll probably be half-asleep in the arena, facing . . . it."

Before Rock could reply, Jansen, reaching for his water glass, said, "I want to propose a toast to the cook, who did a great job for us this time. He served an excellent *final* meal!"

Reelk raised his water glass, too: "Yeah, a toast to the man who served us our last meal."

Nobody laughed. They were all feeling a bit sick. All except Horse-face, who snarled, "Well then, a toast to

106

the Zrano, who'll get us all out of this miserable training—the sooner the better!" His pain-bracelet glinted
in the light as he raised his cup.

The others protested. "What? What are you saying!"

Rockson sighed and said, "How about a toast to the
enjoyment of all the senses? I drink to *pleasure*, gentle-
men. Here's to pleasure, and *NOT* to monsters. We
who are about to die salute *pleasure.*"

He was prepared for a knock at his door some time
around ten o'clock that night, and it came. His dark
hair with the white streak was combed, his welcoming
smile was in place when the door opened. It was
Dovine, not a girl! Rock couldn't say he was pleased.

The fat officer looked around at the neat, bare room
and the pile of books. He didn't make the slightest
personal remark, but said, "I have come to discuss the
request you made to a guard this afternoon, asking for
audi-writing materials."

"Is there any objection? I get women, books, why not
audi-cubes or a pen and some paper at least."

"Not in principle, of course, it's fine. You said that
you wanted the audi-writing to go to your friends on
Earth and Venus?"

"Certainly."

"But why send them anything? To what purpose?"

"So they'll know what happened to me."

"Will they care? Surely they've got their own exist-
ences to plan, their own selves to provide for. They
certainly wouldn't welcome the *taint* of a letter from a
heinous *felon.*"

"They'll care," Rock said. "I was famous back there."

"Even if they want the messages you send it may take
a number of months until the audi-writing can be
delivered. Our rockets don't make many trips in that
direction."

"Am I being told I can't have some means to write

letters?"

"No," Dovine said. "People of influence have given you a great many privileges. I wish that was not the case. However, you will soon face the Zrano, and then," he gleefully slapped the swagger stick on the door frame, "you'll be crushed like a bug!"

Dovine left without formal farewell, his usual habit. Several tiny gray audi-writing squares were brought in shortly afterwards. With the door locked behind him, Rockson pushed the lower toggle of one cube to the left, named the address of his family — the last address he had for them. The material began being printed on the micro-face of the gray square as he began to speak: "This is Rockson here. I may be dead by the time this gets to you." He touched the base of the blue moon lucky medallion at his throat. "Unless a miracle saves me. I won't have died in war, but on account of a retroactive law against playboyism! It's a shame my life should have been so short and that I'll have lost it when I've just started to really enjoy so many wo — *er* — *things*. But I can't complain too much. I've had some very good times and given back a lot of enjoyment to others. I've eaten, drunk, made women happy, and taken the big and small pleasures without hurting anyone — not even myself. That isn't a bad thing to say about somebody who's likely to be dead very soon. Don't think of me the way I'll be when you get this, but the way you knew me. Bless you all." It was short but sweet. Now, if only —

A soft knock came at the door just as he was finishing. He turned as the door was opening on a young girl; his "date" for tonight. She was the best one of all. Still, he was missing Kimetta, traitor and baffler that she was! Kimetta, who had arranged for all sorts of privileges for Rockson.

Rock didn't get any sleep at all.

At daybreak he and the other prisoners were taken out of the building and walked to a jet car that would take them to a special, new arena. This was the day!

Chapter Sixteen

The wide, smooth-running surface vehicle took them past artificial pines and miniplastic hills on the flat asteroid, on toward a huge dome. They were led into the new stadium itself, then down a badly lighted hall to a fair-sized assembly room. Four guards were waiting for them and a door opened on Dovine, as soon as the men had sat down on the marblelike benches.

The sadistic officer started to talk immediately. "I think that all of you are as well prepared as you can be. Except," he smirked, "for Mr. Important." (He meant Rockson.) "Whatever could be done by indoctrination and training has been accomplished. You have your chances. May your skills be equal to the great task."

The mournful prisoners' faces didn't change. They all looked at their punishment bracelets with disgust.

Dovine wasn't finished yet. "A message for Rockson has been sent by my co-worker, Kimetta Langdon." Rock smiled. So the independent-minded young miss who'd helped finger him and bring him here against his will hadn't forgotten his *problem* after all. "Is it a pardon?"

"The message is simply this: 'May the end come quickly,'" Dovine sneered. "That's all."

Rock nodded. "Thank her for me. I'm touched."

Dovine said, "I will; but I personally hope that the end comes *slowly* for *all* of you."

Those were his farewell words.

Silence followed his departure, lasting until Skinny Jones said bitterly, "I wonder if we should find some way to chop off our right wrists, and try to escape."

They were now in a holding area. One of the rather fancy dressed Praetorian honor guards said briskly, "You will soon pick up your weapons, which have been chosen by lot for you. All that remains to be done immediately is for you to choose the order by which you enter the ring." The guard swooped down toward a drawer in the table and reached for a quintet of club-shaped sticks that bulged at one end. Carefully he put them down. "Each will pick one. A cluster of dashes appears on the other side of every stick, and the numerical total will determine the order in which you go into the arena. These ceremonial sticks have been used at every Zrano game for the last thirty years. They're sacred objects."

"Yeah, they're *sacred*," Horse-face repeated caustically, "and life *ain't*."

"When each man chooses a stick he will hold it and not look at the bottom side until the signal is given to do so. That's the rule."

Skinny Jones asked grimly, "And what'll you do if we look right away? Will you punish us by imprisonment until the next games?" No answer.

Horse-face, the first prisoner in line, was directed to reach for a stick, and as he did, he promptly looked at the opposite side.

"Two."

The guard was irritated. "You have broken a tradition." He pressed a button on his metal breast armor and the disobeyer writhed in pain, tearing at his punishment bracelet. After ten seconds, the pain ceased. "Any other wise guys?" sneered the guard.

There were none. After they all got their sticks, they were told to turn them over and count the dashes.

Reelk was staring at the opposite side of his club. "Number four."

Skinny Jones told him eagerly, "That's the *worst* spot because the monster is warmed up. I'm five."

Now Jansen looked at his club. "Three. I'm in the middle."

Rock shrugged and checked his. To his surprise, he too counted three dashes.

"I must have brought a wrong stick," the guard said grabbing it. He went off and started hunting in a side cabinet drawer. "Nothing like it ever happened before," he muttered. He kept shaking his head in disbelief. "It's all cut and dried. How could this have happened?" He finally handed Rockson a number one. "Here, shithead. Wipe off that grin!"

Rock did so.

"First man," the speaker shouted. "You are to leave now for the floor of the arena."

The mournful-looking Reelk turned toward Rock and drew out a hand. "I never told you my first name. I'm Birki. It was a pleasure knowing a playboy. Best kind of crime if you ask me! I was a plumber. Declared retroactively illegal in — I'm *sure* you'll be all right!"

"Thank you for your confidence," Rock said.

They shook hands firmly. "Where's my weapon?" Rock asked.

The guard opened a wide drawer in another synth-oak rolling-cabinet and smirked as he handed Rockson a small tomahawk, the kind you get as a souvenir when you go to a "Wild West" show.

Rock didn't blink as he took it. He had expected this move.

The tall guard that had shocked Horse-face opened the door. A pair of guards in the doorway gestured for Rock to follow. The tall guard closed the door behind him and firmly put his back against it. They were on the floor of the arena, in the glare of TV lights.

There was a big audience. Maybe 100,000 onlookers, all healthy looking, mostly couples. Rockson was expecting a roar of approval or boos from the arena crowd. He heard nothing at all until someone in the first row shouted, "Good luck, sucker."

111

Prisoner Jansen paced back and forth. "What do you think is happening? It's been nearly twenty minutes. Could he still be alive? And what happens if he stays alive? Do we *all* get to go free?"

"It's been twenty minutes since he left," Reelk exclaimed. "I *know* it's been twenty minutes! He made it, I tell you! That playboy lucky-assed bastard made it! And that does mean we go free! It's the rules!"

"Shut up, fool," Skinny Jones said. "He's been gone one lousy minute!"

The walk to the center of the wide dirt floor of the arena took about a minute. A huge clock's sweep second hand — on Rock's right — halfway up in the seats — was counting off the seconds. Rock walked *very* slowly, but when he took more than a minute to get there, his pain-bracelet started egging him on. He moved faster and then stood there with his silly tomahawk. He concentrated fiercely on the huge, closed gate of the Zrano. It didn't come out. Two minutes. What was happening?

At the four-minute mark, the huge death-gate was still shut. The guards who'd been near him suddenly ran away to join the other guards inside the impact-plastic-covered gate he had entered by.

"Walk forward," the speaker shouted. "Face your death bravely."

Chapter Seventeen

Probably the voice was Warden Langdon's. But Rock didn't know or care whose voice that was. He wasn't avid with curiosity to see the Zrano. His skin crawled at the idea, as a matter of fact. The echoing speaker-voice called for him to make the proper salute. He did not raise his arm at first but as pain, like a tearing buzz saw, came through his wristband, he did as requested, raising his tiny tomahawk and saying, "Those of us about to die salute you." He spat up at the warden, who smiled back. The warden was in the first row of the stands, behind plexiglass. Beyond him were seated row after row of shiny-skinned men and women, eager young couples watching his every movement. Two children in the fourth row were open-mouthed.

The wide and sturdy gate at the northeast end of the stadium was still shut, but a sound of pawing came out from behind the gate. Its grooved hasps were held in place by remote control electronic gears, no doubt. What was a Zrano like? Rock found he was interested. A curious reaction. He was dead calm, too. Oddly enough, though he should have felt fear now, he felt *heroic*. And somewhere inside him a tiny voice came: *"You are the Doomsday Warrior. You can conquer this dream. Wake up. Wake up!"* What did the voice mean? Was he going mad?

To his own surprise he was glaring at the dark, woodenlike substance that made up the body of the gate facing him. He heard a series of rhythmic sounds and recognized music, heroic strains. He realized that the audience had risen and was standing rigidly, most of them with their shiny hands flat at their sides. A look out of the corners of his eyes convinced him he was receiving silent *respect* from the audience. He wasn't whining, retreating, or pissing in his boots, like so many others had! They'd never seen that, evidently.

There was a noise that reminded him of nothing he had ever heard before, a slurping and scratchy sound as unlike a human's—or an animal's—as seemed possible. That was when he knew the gate was being raised: when he could hear it.

A turn in that direction showed the gate indeed was rising slowly. The huge dark shape moved forward as the crowd held its breath. He stood and watched as the eighteen-foot-high mass came out into the light. It was surely an extraordinary beast! Three sturdy legs, a thick, chunky body in a most natural tan color—almost like a tree trunk. Six rows of teeth, three facing sets, the middle row like a jagged plank. Three eyes, all red and glowering. The forehead had a single short horn two feet long. It had no hair, not a tuft of hair to be seen—just a few wrinkles on its tan hide. It moved very slowly, forked tongue flicking out as it came clear of the gate. The beast didn't rush out, as it had on the visi-screen in the spacecraft. Probably the Zrano was a little tired of chewing human beings by now. *One could hope!* But its red orb eyes gleamed wickedly. The lust for blood, for death, remained strong in the beast coming toward him. Rockson could sense that.

Rock didn't move. Behind the protective plasti-screen, the audience applauded. Was it for his so-called bravery? For sticking his ground? Or were they urging the *beast* to come at this new prey more quickly? The audience was as fearsome in its way as the Zrano. It seemed if every one would have joined the hunt against him in the arena, with clubs and fists and boots, as if they had been allowed. They *loved* this, Rock realized. Loved to watch this ritual of death. So much the better if he was brave.

The sportsmen kept up their applause as the beast now moved forward, paws outstretched, clawed thumb and two clawed fingers on each of three hands. Apparently the thing would grab him — first.

A voice shouted, "Kill! Kill!"

Rock didn't budge. Now the asteroid-beast wasn't more than ten feet from the tall, muscular warrior. Rockson waited with his own hands far apart. He hadn't moved backwards or looked left or right. It was *amazing* the crowd. The shouts for blood died out. Even the Zrano hesitated, sensing strength.

The beast's steps in his direction were slowed by his opponent's unexpected behavior. Rockson surprised himself by recollecting that he'd never fought anybody in his playboy's easy life. Was he fearless now because the medallion he wore was supposed to keep him safe from all harm? Had it been a joke, and nothing more? Kimetta's little last joke against him, another indignity for a man who was going to die? He brought a hand to his shirt-front, pulled out the blue medallion. The monster focused all its red orbs on the object, froze in place, and seemed to gasp. If such a *big* thing could gasp.

Rockson noticed the medallion's blue gleam catching the lights high above. The beast let out an insane, ear-blasting scream and twisted its head back and forth. It screeched out a long second howl, a wail to make everyone's hair stand on end. The vibration rattled Rockson's rib cage.

He stepped back, unable to stand the sound. There was for a moment an insane temptation in Rockson to let himself be ripped to shreds by the six rows of teeth. And there was also the desire to hold his ears and shut his eyes so that at least he wouldn't hear and see what happened next. To *feel* would be more than enough. Yet he did nothing, neither retreated nor closed his eyes, nor moved forward to attack with his puny weapon. Perhaps, he thought, he just wasn't able to bring himself to miss any part of the last experience he'd ever know. At the sight of what happened next, his eyes widened in disbelief.

The beast *didn't* move forward to eat its helpless prey. Rather, the beast stayed in one place, its body swaying

115

back and forth, trembling. Was there an expression of *fear* in those previously hate-crazed eyes? If that was true, such a switch didn't resemble anything Rock had ever seen or imagined.

Somebody high up in the audience shouted, "What's wrong?"

Rock made it a point to hold the monster's eyes with his own, not sure why it should suddenly be of such great importance. But somehow, he knew it was: a warrior's instinct.

The beast just stood there and gave out pained, hair-raising wails, like a dying elk. It couldn't move at all, it seemed; just its mouth moved. The anguished sounds coming from it went on and on. He was close enough to get the residue of that foul and fearful breath, close enough to wish that the twenty minutes were already finished, one way or the other.

"Get it over," somebody called. "What's going on?"

The creature now began to shake and actually whimper, and kept walking backward, away from him, in the direction of the gate.

The crowd's roar became confused, and as Rockson stamped his feet and walked after the beast, threatening it with his silly toy axe, they all erupted into applause. It was homage to the brave, tall Earthman who moved forward confidently while the Zrano stumbled away, homage to a playboy turned warrior.

The clock rang out twenty minutes. It was over. The Zrano went into its gate, the gate shut back. Rockson's life had been spared. He wished he knew how it had happened. He had an idea it was the medallion. He bowed and raised his hand in the V-for-victory salute. The warden took off his laurel-wreath hat and threw it over the plexiglass and into the arena. Rockson put it on.

A nightmare had turned into a pleasant dream!

Chapter Eighteen

After Rockson made many, many bows, the same blond guard who had taken care of him before took Rock, via a circuitous route, out to a small grav-car. The guard drove him "home," back to the room he had been given. On the way, the guard said, "Maybe the others think you're a hero. But I know you're not. I know how you did it!"

"How?"

The guard explained it. Rockson was amazed at what had caused his good fortune.

There was a knock, much later. Before Rock said anything, the door opened, revealing Dovine. The officer's perpetually disapproving look seemed frozen on that immobile, flaccid face. He wasn't happy. That was an understatement. "You are only the third survivor in the history of the games! You are to be congratulated. How did you pull it off? You can tell me. There is an immutable law that you must not die now. Unfortunately, you will have to be released."

"How soon can I get away from this asteroid?"

Dovine smiled. "You will be released *on* this asteroid, not *off*. That's all! You will *never* leave this tiny world. You live, that is all. There is only one condition to your claiming this "freedom": You *must* tell me how you did it—how you defeated the Zrano. I am recording your answer now, on an audi-cube, for review of the council. Tell *them!*"

"OK," Rock sighed. "The medallion I wear had a picture of the Zrano's *mother* on it, in a spectrum we humans can't see. It got all shook up—guilty, if you will. I freaked it out."

"Really? I doubt that anyone had ever thought that a picture of its mother would make a Zrano back down. How did you know *that* Rockson?"

"It's the last of its kind. It hasn't seen its mother since it was a little thing just out of its egg. It is usual that a child, especially an only child, remembers and misses its dead mother. I was taking a guess, but my guess was right."

"Where did you get the medallion? What traitor gave it to you?"

Rock lied, not wanting to implicate Kimetta. "I found it jammed in a crevice in a rock formation near the spaceport. When we landed."

Dovine seemed partly satisfied. He pondered for a time and said, "Yes. I see . . . contestants *have* been allowed to take harmless-looking fetishes into the ring with them, good luck charms. I have heard of these old souvenir medallions, like yours. Cheap holograms of the first Zranos. The people here don't have any super-stitious toys now, not being able to spare the time from work to indulge in pernicious nonsense. They surely threw away many such trinkets from the old days. Thank you Rockson. Thank you for reinstating my belief in your cowardice! Never again will a contestant be allowed to carry *anything* into the arena except his lot-weapon!"

Rock nodded sadly, seeing in his mind the next poor victim of the Zrano's wrath. "Yes, I think I understand that. I guess I'm lucky!"

Dovine nodded. "So much so that you're about to be visited by the council head, Esmerelda's great *Panxux* himself."

Rock remembered the furrowed brow and irritable look of the man who had occupied a cloth-draped box in the second row at the arena, the man sitting behind the warden when the warden had given him the laurel crown he still wore. "When is the Panxux coming here?"

118

"Soon. He wants to congratulate you Rockson, and help make arrangements for your future. The warden has no power over you now. You're no longer a convict!"

"All he has to do is get me on a space rocket, and that'll be all the future of mine I can care about."

Dovine said, "Fat chance. Be happy if he doesn't find something else nasty for you. You survived the Zrano, let's see if you can survive meeting Panxux. He's — quite changeable. A fruitcake, some say. You will see. Goodbye!"

A few moments after these words, an impatient knock led to the door's being opened quickly. The man who walked in at the front of a small group was smaller than Rockson would have guessed from the stadium. His chin was not as assertive as it had seemed. Yet the eyes were the same, wide apart and darkly feral, and the lips as generously twisted.

"My congratulations and those of all Esmerelda!" Panxux spoke out clearly and robustly, shaking Rock's hand. "You shall be permitted to live out your days with us in peace and honor as a citizen first class!"

"I don't want that. I have the right to leave, according to the rules."

"Are you not a criminal? You would just be rearrested on Venus and sent back! Only here is your 'rehabilitation' recognized!"

"I am a playboy. That used to be legal. I was railroaded."

"You're now respected on Esmerelda. Why do you want to leave? There is much you haven't seen here. Very interesting pleasant jobs will be offered to you. The women will please you."

"I know as much about this asteroid as I'd like to know, ever. And work of any kind doesn't suit me, really," Rockson picked at his nails. "I insist on leaving."

"But you haven't seen it all!"

"Nothing about this asteroid is worth knowing!"

119

"Not true." The voice was growing unpleasantly whining. If he had been an Earthman, Rock would have guessed the ruler's age at about forty, but now he sounded like a spoiled infant. He raged, "On this asteroid *everybody* has to work in order to survive! In your case, you will be offered a good option. You can run a large industry, a factory of any kind at all!"

"I have an option to leave: that's the one I want to take," Rock insisted. "I read the rules. Over in *that* pile of books." Rockson pointed at his mass of night readings.

The council head sighed. "There are certain problems of which you might not be aware," Panxux said calmly. "To start, a supply rocket doesn't take off until the end of the month. Twenty more day-night units."

"I want to be on it, as soon as it arrives. I have the right."

"Passage has been strictly apportioned out among diplomats, trade mission people, and vital cargo. There isn't room for any luxury cargo like you. We didn't — anticipate — your survival, you see. I suspect the warden's daughter's hand in *that*."

"*When* will there be room?" Rockson wanted to keep off the subject of Kimetta.

"Perhaps four or five cargo runs from now."

Rock sighed. "I want to be on the first available rocket in that case."

"Yes. I see . . . well, you are a cool customer aren't you? A tough cookie! It will be attended to, *if* you insist. But the wait will be very very long. You will go on a tour of Esmerelda in the meanwhile. Maybe you will decide to stay."

"I *might* take a tour, since I have time. I'll relax and go on a tour. But *don't* welsh on me. I can be bad luck to cross. Remember the Zrano!"

If Rock hadn't known better, he'd have sworn that the ruler of Esmerelda had blinked at the threat. Then Panxux laughed, long and hard. "Say you *are* a corker!

What work will you accept in the meantime?"

"None. I will just tour around, if that's OK."

"But how will you earn your food and board? You need credits now. Say, didn't you once have a managerial job? Wasn't that in your file?"

"I never have." The comic remarks that surged to Rock's lips remained unspoken. "I never worked. Not ever," he insisted.

Panxux smiled again. "What a strange man you are! Not before this have I encountered anybody who lived to your age without having done any work. Don't you want to be socially useful?"

"I consider that many of the things I've done are socially useful. The women think so."

Panxux didn't follow that up directly, but Dovine put in, over a concealed mike, "I believe he refers to his well-known and many relations with women. He claims to have made many women happy. Indeed Rockson has been with one A-1 each and every night since arriving here. A different A-1 every night."

"But where is the usefulness in that?" Panxux shrugged at Rock. "You may have an interesting philosophy, but it is bankrupt, Rockson. I don't have the wish or the time for a long conversation about your bankrupt philosophy."

Rock told him quietly, "You might be a better person if you did think about something more than toil on occasion."

"Of course I might," Panxux agreed surprisingly, "but I'm *far* too busy. My question is this: What do you mean by saying that to make a woman happy can be socially useful?"

"I'm not sure I know the full answer, myself," Rock admitted. "But let a man make a woman happy and he'll be happy himself. If they're workers, they can work better as a result of a certain amount of mutual pleasure in sex."

"You're saying that to make bed with a woman is

121

enough to sustain social usefulness?" Panxux shook his head fiercely. "*Not* here. If you knew this planetoid better, you'd agree. When you tour, you will understand, and then, I am sure, you will want to stay. I'm *certain* of it!"

"To do something nice for another human being is itself useful, I say."

Panxux, with a wave of the hand, dismissed the subject. "The matter had been fully discussed. During the next five or six months, while you wait for a space ride," Panxux said, "you will be studied by a group of our leading scientists and theorists and scholars. Their reports ought to be of some interest to the council — perhaps giving us all better knowledge of the latent criminality in some *earthlings*. An insight into the great crime of laziness."

Rock ignored the racial slur. "But you'll still put me on a supply rocket, see that I'm reserved for it?"

"Yes, provided you will assist our studies. Is that clear?"

Without waiting for an answer, the ruler started to the door. Watching his swagger intently, Rock realized how much the two of them really shared. Each was intelligent and opinionated, each was willing to talk from a point of wary mutual respect, a respect that shaded into a liking of sorts. But there was yet something else that the two of them shared: at no time would either be able to understand the other!

Rockson had a bad dream again that night, the worst yet. He dreamed that some strange clone of Dovine's by the name of Zhabnov buried Rockson alive.

Chapter Nineteen

One month later:

A man in a gray lab smock got up and addressed the twelve-man Esmereldan council. "Rockson has seen the mines, and refused work there. He has been studied for a month," said Dr. Kreister, the philo-scientist, as he directed his piercing black eyes toward Panxux in particular. "Four months approximately are left until Rockson leaves us. Four months during which he will continue to be totally useless, taking up needed air and space and eating precious tiblets. Tiblets that only *workers* deserve. No work, no air! And he affects women in a bad way. Makes them rebellious."

Panxux's lips were briefly pursed. "So you suggest — ?"

"That he be put to death," the scientist said. "I see no other alternative. The rulebook allows for exceptions under emergency situations. Rockson is an emergency."

Rock, who had been summoned to attend the meeting, was not happy with its first pronouncements. He stood up from his place in the back of the large meeting room and shouted, "Dammit, you can't change the rules! Listen to me too!"

Panxux frowned. "No time. Sorry! I've allotted twenty-two minutes for a deposition of this matter. We can't hear you." Panxux's eyes were back on the scientist. "You may continue, noble Doctor Kreister."

The gray-bearded man smiled and spoke on crisply. Rock was held at riflepoint by a guard, and with his pain-bracelet "heating up," couldn't speak, couldn't disagree with anything. All human feelings were left out of what the doctor was saying. Facts were slanted against him. The conclusion was that Rockson should be sent to the "Bureau of Corrections." The council agreed.

He was brought by compu-car to the looming, blue, glass building and deposited in a room that was comfortable without being an inch larger than what was needed to contain eight chairs, a small room off the largest corridor. After five hours, he met Ezlin and half a dozen other Esmereldans concerned with "correction." Twenty minutes into the long examination of his papers, Ezlin called for a decision.

"What do you think of Rockson?" Ezlin asked. "According to Dr. Kreister, the Earthman doesn't use his eyes for work or study, just for pleasures. His hands and shoulders and arms are developed oddly — as in somebody who has sex, not somebody who works. I'd agree and say that Rockson isn't ever likely to be a worker. He must be corrected surgically."

Rockson didn't like *that* statement one bit! He would have dived out the window, but the bracelet sent a paralyzing drug into his veins, and a warning pain.

Broomak, the liberal among the red-tunicked men, suggested, "We can perhaps do without surgery. We must show him how different types of work are done and by whom, and try to change his mind. Give him a great choice."

"You won't succeed," Ezlin said, "but you may try."

Much relieved, a tired Rockson was taken to the home of a contented factory worker, a man supposedly at ease with his women and their children. Rock was startled at the tiny room in an apartment complex that the three women, three children, and one husband lived in.

"Do all of you live here?" Rock asked, Broomak looking on.

"Of course," the husband said. "This unit is twelve by fourteen. The roof is made of soft warm glassov and the floor is polywood. The toilet is under the bed — it pops out, as do six bunks from the wall. We have to conserve space, do what's best for the community. We manage, as long as we can work."

Rock was still muttering when Broomak took him on to a portahouse, a complex with a dozen so-called detach-homes put down one on top of another. The units could be, he said, dismantled, unstacked at will, and taken somewhere else by crane. They used a key to go in an empty ground-floor unit.

"How big is each of these units?" Rock asked.

"Seventeen by sixteen, on average. Bigger than the one you saw, but the family units are larger."

"That's what I'd have guessed."

They went into a small utility bathroom, equipped with a jet-shower. Broomak was proud of the feature, a new one.

"But what about the ordinary comforts of living?" Rock asked. "A sink for instance."

"The sink is unnecessary as there is a shower."

"I don't notice a compu-range for cooking."

"The range and freezall and visi-screen are part of the same unit, stored under the bed. This unit will service three one-man, two-women units with nine children."

Rock nodded. He had been reading about the multi-partner Esmereldan family units. The work in the mines was dangerous, and families that lost husbands or wives were by law absorbed by other families, according to some sort of lottery. "How can living beings live like this, after working as hard as these people do?" Rock asked. He felt suffocated, boxed in.

"Like all of us," Broomak said, "they have to conserve space and energy. Each person here is a work unit, no more. Except the children under five years old." Broomak raised a bushy black eyebrow. "Your responses are intensely interesting from an academic point of view, but you have not a very practical mind. I would hate to lose such a fine specimen as you!"

"What next?"

"I'll continue showing you the importance that we

Esmereldans attach to work, Rockson. I have faith that all men, even you, will see that work is its own reward."

A compu-car took them through a stretch of flat land with artificial trees and metallic birds imitating life in the artificial air. At a robotoid factory, producing, as part of a trade agreement, spare parts for androids on Venus and Alpha Centauri Four, the thin-lipped officer in charge escorted them along the noisy work floor. A lot of arc-welding was going on.

"After my time here," he told Rockson, "I go home for an hour with my women and boy-child, then have a meal, and go out to my other job—I am a miner in pit 397-691."

"You've got *two* jobs?"

"I used to have three, but found myself falling asleep at odd times and had to give up one of them."

"Do you need credits so much?"

"I work for the pleasure of occupying additional waking time. What's there in life except work—and the arena-games, of course?"

Rock wanted to say that he'd never understand such a point of view. The man was staring at a point down the line of parts makers, where there was a jam-up. The lapse was handled by somebody, and he relaxed.

"What was your other job?" Rock asked. "The third one?"

"Oh, I worked at the human factory."

"The *what?*"

"The place where—oh, dammit!" The small man wheeled and ran down the line of parts makers, shouting. Broomak took Rock from there as soon as it dawned on him that the wait for the worker to return was likely to be a long one.

"I should think a man like that one would have a breakdown," Rock said as they got in their car.

"Breakdown? Here?" Broomak tapped his shiny forehead. "The possibility is handled nicely on this asteroid. I'll show you, if you think you'd be interested.

Maybe . . . yes, maybe you'll be interested to work in *that* section: *mind-preservation.*"

"I'd like to *look* at what you do about mental health," Rock said evasively.

Broomak made some computations in the computer under the car's steering wheel. The compu-car diverted, took them through a silent stand of artificial trees and under a waterfall with liquid shooting down in color sprays. Not real — a hologram.

Shortly, Broomak eased the car down into a slot by a small, white-painted shingle building. Inside, twenty men and women were sitting stiffly on chairs; the nearest woman had a pained look on her shiny features. Rock's smile wasn't returned. He looked for some possible cause besides bad manners, and saw that the woman's hands had been tied to the plastex arms of the chair, her waist to the chair back.

"What's wrong with her? With all of these people?"

Broomak said, "Mental instability. But that will be fixed." He pressed a button labeled Therapy. Voltage shot into devices in the seats. The strapped-in victims started jerking and they repeated, "I feel well, I feel *perfectly* well. I want to go back to work, to both of my jobs, very soon, very soon." They kept repeating it.

Rock whirled on Broomak. "Is *this* what you do to anybody who says he's had enough? You tie them down and shoot them full of electricity so they do nothing except recite bullcrap? Is that it?"

"Look, Rockson," said his guide, "this is nothing compared to the next room. That's reserved for prisoners like you, people who don't accept jobs, don't accept limits on freedom. You've got friends in high places, but once the council gives up on you — you'll be *corrected*, I warn you!"

For a second Rock had some sort of weird déjà vu. He pictured himself in the same sort of contraption — only with a headset — and needles, hot needles going into his brain. A mind-fucker machine? Something like that! And he was, in this vision, in another place, another reality entirely. There in the other world's coffin machine was *himself*, but he wasn't a playboy-prisoner. He was a hero, known as the DOOMSDAY WARRIOR! A man in deep, deep shit trouble!

Broomak, who'd been watching Rock's face with a look of anxious curiosity, asked, "What else would you suggest? It gets them back to work. They don't remember this anyway."

"What about — er — vacations for them?" Rock's head was swimming.

"There's too much work to be done," Broomak bristled. "Everybody who wakes up with a headache or nosebleed would soon be demanding a vacation."

"Once a year, at least. It could be a big help," Rock said.

"Do you know what happens to men and women on a vacation? They spend all the time hating each other and their families. They play too much and then become ill. Many a man or woman has become deathly ill in the course of a vacation, as you call it, and many have died as a result."

"Many people *don't* die as a result, but are able to do better work when they come back."

"People are bitterly unhappy during the vacation periods, I'm telling you; it hurts production. On Esmerelda there's hardly enough of anything to go around. We live on a frontier of the galaxy. This is a hard life, and every possible area of productivity must be pushed forward."

Rock nodded slowly. "I think I can understand that, but I can't understand this sort of therapy. Maybe production could be better if people were allowed freedom."

"I take it," the official said, "you don't want to work here? All you have to do is feed them and turn the therapy on and off — and some paperwork."

"I'd rather not!"

"We ought to leave then. Next, Rockson, you'll see the—"

"I'm too tired. I've been up for thirty-six hours at least. I need rest. I feel—strange."

"Where do you want to go?"

"The place where I'm living. The room in the first arena, I suppose."

Broomak allowed him to do so.

He ate dinner by himself, a primitive meal not remotely like what he'd been fed when he was expected to go up against the monster. And no prosti-women knocked on the door. He sat up thinking: to have any value placed on a human life here would require a revolution. Maybe he'd start one!

After he'd been asleep a short while there was a knock on the door.

The spectacularly built strawberry blond girl who walked into his room wore a mask. She smiled coolly and said to him, "Kimetta sent me. I'm Ronette, her twin sister."

"You look a *lot* like her."

"We are to have sex," she said. "Now." She stripped off all her outer clothes, then her bra, and her panties. "I prefer to do all the work in the sex act—OK?"

Chapter Twenty

"Don't you want to talk a little bit first?" But Rockson felt his manhood erupting, despite his tiredness.

"There's no reason for it," she said, ripping his blanket away.

He smiled and nodded, then, "I don't suppose that's a no." He lay back and enjoyed it, suspecting strangely that this was not a twin, but the *real* Kimetta, Kimetta playing games.

Within an hour, he had to take another tiblet. He was out of breath.

"Excuse me," he complained, "but I'm not a machine intended for pleasure. I—have to think. Alone. Something *wrong*."

Only a sharp look from "Ronette" proved that she had retained some human sensibilities. "If you've got any new ideas for sex, we'll do it. If you've never thought of it before, think of it now. And don't be shy. Kimetta said to give it *all* to you."

He did think of something new, and she complied. Even in the "Venusian Arc-Monster position," her body fitted very snugly against his.

The next few minutes passed in almost a dreamlike state as far as he was concerned. She was ready for what he wanted, her body fine-tuned to please, left leg raised, lowered, raised. He had only to indicate, to gesture, and it was done for him as he craved. She was better than Kimetta (or if she was Kimetta, she'd been practicing). *Or the dream was getting better.* Crazy thought!

They slept in one another's arms. When he awoke before the masked girl, he started to kiss her, to touch her lightly until the shiny skin tingled in his hands and against the tips of his fingers. He wasn't impatient, but took his time and explored the hollows and curves, the breasts and the flat stomach. She moaned, half-awake. He drew a deep breath to smell the warmth of her skin so close to him.

The girl's big blue eyes opened. Even with the Lone Ranger-type mask on, she looked amazed. Then she reached out, embracing him as if for dear life. Slowly, her hands and lips and tongue began to respond, to join him in avid exploration, in the giving and receiving of mutual pleasure. This time it was different than last night. It was tender.

"Now," she called in a different voice, "now, *now!*"

He rose above her and they moved back and forth together in the fullness of mutual pleasure, until she cried out in release.

Later, as they lay all sweated up, smoking the Pall Mall cigarettes she had brought along in her purse, she opened up finally: Ronette talked about her work at the prosti-service. Her job was simple: she was a Class A-1 woman, a clone of Kimetta's. She would make bed with a man, like all the other unattached women on Esmerelda, for credits paid by the asteroid government. Only if the transaction had the government's approval of course. She couldn't pick her partners. "Only *real* women like Kimetta Langdon can *pick* their sex partners."

"Why?"

"The man has to be worthy of the relaxation, that's why."

"It doesn't sound great," he commented. "Do you ever get a vacation?"

She didn't even know what it meant. "I haven't heard of that," she shrugged. "Is 'vacation' a good position?"

"No, I don't suppose there are vacations around here," he muttered.

Ronette, looking at the alarm clock, said, "I have been in this room longer than any other time I've been

131

sent to service a man. It is time for me to go."

But she stood slowly, dressed slowly, and said softly, "You must ask for me again. They allow preferences. I'm K-51 Ronette. Don't forget."

"I won't."

"Is that a promise?"

"Of course."

Not until after Ronette had left and he was relocking his door, did Rock turn toward the bureau and see a ten-credit note. He had been on Esmerelda long enough to recognize the square piece of red glow-paper. His smile ended, he flushed deeply. He found himself feeling sorry for that delightful girl. She had made bed with many males, but had enjoyed herself only once.

And the only sure way she knew to show that enjoyment was to *pay* him!

Chapter Twenty-one

Rockson was taken out to a parts factory that day, in what he thought of as the morning. After his first long look around he wished he had never gone to the place. He wondered what was going to happen to him if he didn't take a job soon, though.

The large building, three stories tall, was unpainted concrete, a *blank* from the outside. The "receiving room" was large and wide, with head-high file cabinets. A prim, brunette woman in a gray nurse's outfit sat behind a desk the shape of a lima bean and filled out audi-writing cubes by micropen. The cubes were then deposited into one of the ten-drawer cabinets opening ten on a side. There were millions of cubes already filed.

"Why did you want me to see this?" Rock asked, more loudly than he had expected. "What is this place?"

"Sort of a morgue," Broomak admitted. "Come see."

Rock's throat seemed to catch as the "nurse" let them into a well-lighted, vast, white room. A man in a gray smock was standing beside a table on which a bluish human corpse lay. The corpse's eyes had been removed and put onto a bed of soft plasti-seal material. Another man in a smock was sawing off the body's legs, while a third checked out nasal passages with a small machine that dilated the nostrils. For a second, Rockson thought the corpse was *himself*.

"Deviated septum," that man mumbled into a recorder. "No use for that. What about the sexual parts?"

The first man in gray consulted the section of audi-writing in his hand. "Excellent condition, but there's no need for penis transplantation anywhere at this time;

we'll store it, all the same. I want a report on the liver and kidneys and spleen and stomach, Henry. The heart problem killed him, so we do without that. He's been hearted before, hasn't he?"

"A transplant only twelve weeks ago, the second, after his third attack. This guy couldn't get used to the residues in the air at his L-Kromide factory. Allergy, I guess."

A buzzer sounded twice.

"Oh hell, I have a new patient. Henry, you finish with the testicles right away. I don't want to busy with this one any longer."

As the assistant started removing the parts, Rock couldn't prevent the tension that made him cup both palms over his crotch. "I'm getting out of here," he whispered, and Broomak and he went back to the file room.

The nurse looked up and smiled. They rushed past and Rock was surprised to see the bearded Ezlin himself waiting outside the main door.

"That's the one place even I myself find it hard to stay in," Ezlin confessed, drawing a deep breath. "It's all that talk about transplanting livers and spleens that disturbs me."

"I guess each of us is disturbed by different things," Rock remarked. "I didn't know a parts factory meant human parts."

"It occurred to me that you might not feel so sensitive, and could consider working here. I see that I was wrong."

"You surely were," Rock considered. "I'd rather work with the living."

"A nobler sentiment would be to collect spare parts for the needy."

Had the usually controlled Ezlin stooped to sarcasm?

"I can be noble."

"Let's see if that's true. Broomak—take him to the Life School. If he doesn't want that job—you've failed and—." Ezlin threw up his hands.

"Fine."

For a moment Rockson and Broomak seemed to like each other, because it was obvious neither liked Ezlin.

The Life School was a five-story, unpainted building without windows. Lots of blanks on this planetoid!

There were sounds of raised voices as they stepped out of the compu-car. A square door burst open, and a dozen men and women in pink tights and no tops rushed out to the artificial air. One of the young men was being pelted by all the others' clenched fists.

"*What* is this?" an outraged Broomak demanded sharply. "Why are you all wasting time?"

A buxom, bare-breasted girl answered, "It's *his* fault! He is responsible for making our lives a living Earth!" But now the entire entourage stopped and quieted down.

Rock didn't smile at hearing the name of his home planet used as another word for hell. All the same, he'd keep this memory for quite a while. The petite blond bounced wonderfully.

"What's he done?" Broomak demanded.

"Among other things," she fumed, "Breel-49 kept some important audi-writing out from the library for six weeks." She glowered at the young, finely built male wilting under her glare. "When he was forced to give it back, he had x'ed out important write-parts that would have helped other students of the Life School!"

Another young man said, "And I myself caught him breathing on a culture in a lab experiment of mine, so it wouldn't work out right. I *caught* Breel-49, do you hear?"

"That's even more despicable." Broomak glared. He evidently felt more respect for lab work than library material. "You deserve whatever these fellow-students do to you, Breel-49—continue!"

135

The guilty student tried to run, but was pulled to the ground and pummeled as Rock and Broomak walked on into the building.

"Students fight each other for unfair advantages in the name of hard work," Broomak said. "It makes for resourceful members of the community. Competition is godly."

"No it isn't."

"I'm sorry Rockson, if your ethical concepts are being shaken. Or should I say *un*ethical concepts!"

Inside the plain building was a corridor lined with doors. They went inside a classroom. It was empty, but there were book-machines and piles of audi-cubes on each of a hundred desks.

"Here the young study the history of work, to develop the logic inescapable, derived by the great Foncluson Klossam himself. The great statement that nothing in this universe matters except work."

"That's the Life School?"

"That's it! Do you think you could be a proctor here? Good work for an intellectual man of the galaxy! And you get to study the words of Klossam!"

"Rather not," Rock said. "Hate School."

"You are incorrigible! Well—maybe I'll give you *one* last chance to find employment, Rockson. Do you think you'd like to see the police forces at work? You might understand why certain security measures are necessary, might want to join them for your stay here."

"I wasn't meant to hold people down, even if what they're doing is wrong," Rock said. "Others can do that, but not me. I'm no cop!"

Broomak began to sputter and redden. He said, "*Very* well, *then*."

Broomak paused, once they got in the compu-car, with a hand over the destination slot beneath the wheel. "Do you have *any* opinion about what you'd like to see? I've been consistently wrong. You might be able to solve the problem of work *yourself*."

Rock considered a long time. "I'd like to see *little* kids. I don't think that, even here, kids want pain."

"Perhaps you'd like to teach small children?"

"Maybe I would." Rock didn't add, *"before it's too late."* Maybe he could do a little good on this damned work-asteroid after all in the few months he'd be staying.

The compu-car took them to a very large, purple-and red-spotted building set in a grove with three others of the same seven-story size. It looked like a set of crazed-out beehives! The sign on the buildings Rock saw filled him with a long moment's unhappiness. "Busy Bee Schools? Oh *no!*" He added, "No windows?"

"There isn't any need to distract the children," Broomak said. "Come on—let's go into a school unit."

A ramp took them up to a narrow door by electric power. A chance for the happy playboy to exercise his feet again!

In a well-lit classroom, a robot looked out at sixty bald-shaven boys and girls, all about six years old. Rock was struck by their quiet, by the absence of rustling or whispering. Were they doped up?

"Now you will take out your audi-writings," the ro-bo-teacher said. "You will turn to the first blank section after yesterday's lesson."

Noises this time, but not many. The children moved with the minimum of fuss and stirring. Rock, who'd never seen anything like it from youngsters, just stared.

"You will audi-write the following," the robo-teacher began. When the robot spoke, there was a hard sound of the words being repeated by all the youngsters, like a responsive reading in church, said without meaning. They were repeating, of course, some words by the work-mad philosopher, Klossam.

"What *is* all this?" Rock couldn't help asking. "Those kids look and sound like they've been programmed—is anything wrong with them? Why the hair shaved off?"

"Of course they are quiet. This is *work*. They should all look and sound alike. Why not?"

"They are being turned into zombies! Don't tell me something hasn't been done to them! I've seen healthy kids learning their lessons, and it's nothing like this! They must be drugged!"

Broomak took it on himself once more to explain in quiet tones, "On Esmerelda we've eliminated nonsense from children by giving them Barlox-39 in their tiblets. Barlox-39 makes them calm and attentive over a twenty-four-hour period. They go to sleep when told, they recite when told—always well behaved. At age eight years, they're switched to Koors-Connets pills for a full twelve months, which allows for memorizing jobs with complex responsibility. After that, they're considered to be fully grown citizens, and they're sent to work."

"You're turning the kids into monsters!"

"No, quite the contrary. They escape unpleasant 'squirmy' phases that children on other planets and asteroids have to go through; the pains of growing up are avoided."

"But people have to be *alive,* to go through *phases.* You can't take away from children the right to live through a normal phase, even though it's a hard one. When you do that, you force them to be less alive. It's worse than uncivilized."

"We can't afford to waste time with children in emotional difficulties," Broomak insisted. "Every child is a needed unit."

"Every child is *important.* Everyone is *unique!*"

Broomak pointed out sadly, "Ezlin and the council are right. You *never* will agree."

"That's the best thing you could have said to me."

"You reject life, when you reject order," Broomak recited from the Book of Kossam. "I doubt your high-placed girlfriend can help you now, you, you ingrate!"

138

Chapter Twenty-two

Rockson again faced the council. Ezlin received Broomak's admission that he had failed to "correct" Rockson. He nodded and reached down to raise a visi-screen from a lower shelf. He flipped through images. "We've exhausted every resource but one — aside from execution. One last chance, Rockson. You might want to work in the area that provides *pleasure* for the people of Esmerelda."

"That sounds — interesting," Rock said automatically, feigning interest. "That's it! That's the work I'd like to do! You thought of it, at long last."

Ezlin smiled. "You will begin your job as trainer right n —"

Then Rock looked wary. "Wait just a minute! I've only heard of *one* pleasure that Esmereldans share. The so-called games!"

"Correct, and I feel that room can be made for arena employment by someone as interested as you in improving the quality of life here!"

With a flick of the visi-screen dial, Ezlin turned on the image, a picture unmistakably clear. A photograph of the death-arena appeared. The ritual of death it seemed had started once again. The Zrano was recovered from Rockson's attack of gloom. The deadly gate was opening, a mortally frightened man stood on the sands of despair. There was a pause for the stadium audience to bid him farewell. The lumbering nightmare-beast charged to kill.

Rockson couldn't keep his eyes from the screen, despite his disgust. He was hardly aware that Ezlin was now talking to him, saying, "If you want to improve the games, you have a good chance to do it, in your new job."

"What do you mean?" Rock watched the victim make a run for it. He was young and ran very fast in a zig-zag, but the Zrano kept at his heels. Three legs were faster than two. A psychotic, multitoothed piano stool versus a mere human.

"You of all people can surely think of some ways to ease the strain on the gladiators' lives. I feel that you might be interested—"

"Here he comes!" an older council member suddenly called out. "The Zrano's got him now!"

"Looks worried," another councilman shouted, gleefully.

"Worse than that. Petrified," another laughed.

Ezlin asked Rock, "How *does* it feel out there, knowing that you're facing death? I mean how does it *really* feel inside?"

Rock said nothing. The Zrano closed its jaws on the victim, swallowing the man's scream.

Rock looked away.

Getting to his feet slowly, Rock planned on talking to these men quietly, making them understand what their evil system was doing to other humans. But they were enraptured by the pictures of the man dying. Almost before he realized what he was doing, he knocked the visi-screen to the floor. It shattered.

Ezlin stood up, shouting, "You can't do that!"

"Watch me!" Nothing else was left of Rock's planned speech on decency and morality—only those two grim words.

As he stepped on the pieces of the visi-screen, satisfying crunches came to Rock's ears, more like old-fashioned wood splintering than any glassov. He was standing on the fading picture of the frightened man, grinding it to pieces under him. The scream continued. It took longer to trample the wirecord for sound.

All the Esmereldan councilmen were standing in silent outrage. Only Ezlin, briefly on his feet, returned

140

to his seat and was staring in a disconcerting way at Rock.

"I felt sure you would take the arena job," the bearded scientist said. "After all, you've had direct experience of the games and have expressed some interest about the things that give pleasure to others."

"Pleasure?" He drew a deep breath. "Pain for others *isn't* pleasure! Is that really so hard for you all to understand?"

"You will be taken back to your room," Ezlin sighed. "I think we've all seen enough of you. There is obviously no hope for you. I wash my hands now. Heavens, how I tried!"

And at that moment Rock was reminded of how he had felt the first time he'd seen the Zrano on a visi-screen. A flick of fear coursed through his body. He would have run, but the very thought started the pain-bracelet to punishing him with bolts of pain. Somehow, he would face the pain.

Run where?

Where does a man in a box run?

Chapter Twenty-three

The sentence was execution. Tomorrow. Back in his guarded room, Rock found the answer to his dilemma on his bureau — the inspiration was the ten-credit cash-note from Ronette!!

When the guards came to lead him to the execution chamber, Rock said, "Tell the council I will accept a job!"

They looked disconcerted but went away, locking him back in.

A short time later, Rock faced Ezlin in Ezlin's study.

"Are you jerking me around?" a tired Ezlin asked.

"No."

"What job would you like to perform? This I've *gotta* hear!"

Rock replied, "It occurs to me that if the women of Esmerelda were more pleased with their bed partners, it could bring on a state of general happiness that would increase their production."

"Yes, I'm sure." Ezlin looked suspicious. "Tell me, then, what work you would seriously suggest for yourself? There's not much time before we execute —"

"It occurred to me late last night that I'd like to show on a visi-screen how it is possible for a man and a woman to be happy making love," Rock said. "I can record my — er — encounters with the prosti-women. Show other men how to — er — *do it!* Sex is as natural as sleeping and eating, and you wouldn't, I'm sure, hesitate to show those other functions on a visi-screen." Rockson really *didn't* intend to make sex tapes. He had a *plan.*

"I see . . . interesting, but the visi-screens are hardly watched, except during the Zrano games. And there are five games this week. . . ."

"Then knock the games off the air!"

"No, we can't do that." Ezlin looked down at his folded hands. "The games cause universal pleasure, and to halt them is to invite a rebellion, or at least hurt production."

"Postpone the games, and *increase* production! You need more production don't you? Everyone here is on a bare sustenance diet, aren't they? Even you!"

The weary man said softly, "I think you have an idea, but the video if O-U-T! The next best thing would be to use audi-writing. Do a manual on lovemaking, Rockson. That'll be your new job! You will be a writer! No correction of your mind necessary—OK?"

"No! There are already manuals on the mechanics of making love. I remember reading one in my room. And manuals, obviously," Rockson went on, "don't seem to work, as far as your women are concerned!" Rock was picking his words carefully. "The girls think that sex is unpleasant or just a work duty they've got to be paid for! It shouldn't be like that. There can be joy in it for each, warmth and pleasure. And *happiness* increases *work!* Let me do the videos!"

"And who'd pay attention to advice on making sex from a young man whose only claim to fame here is that he survived an encounter with the Zrano?"

"There would *certainly* be some interest if you publicized my crime. Remember, I'm the *greatest playboy in the galaxy!*"

"It might work." The Esmereldan's generous lips quirked at the corners. "You have a fresh idea; go tell Panxux."

Soon Rockson presented his case to Panxux, the council leader: "Sir, allow me to work at the job I'm best at!" Rock *had* him there. It was against the laws of Klossam to deny a man work that he was good at!

"I think you'd have to understand that my schedule is an imposing one," the man, trying not to agree, said. "These few minutes spent on the matter of your future is the first free time I've had in many a long month, and now I must go!"

"You didn't answer me. I demand the job! And I need to do it with Kimetta. She's the best!"

"Despite how randy you may be, Rockson, I can assure you that this asteroid doesn't need an official pornographer!" He glared. "A royal pornographer so to speak!"

"Not even if the point is that the porno increases production? The great philosopher stated, "The good is what —"

"Improves production," the council leader sighed. "You win! You have your job. To my dying day, I will *never* believe that I took part in any conversation like this! But we've been without wars, thanks to Klossam. A program of unceasing work is the answer for preventing mass slaughter."

Rock snapped, "Or it might be that the slaughter of a few people in an arena makes others stop thinking about —"

"Fuck! Go make your damned pictures, Rockson! That will be all! I'll advise the council the execution is *off*." Showing Rock out, the leader of Esmerelda opened the door on a surprise.

A man stood in that door, lights glinting off the tip of a grav-knife he was carrying tightly in his right hand, which was raised. The leader backed off, so that he was alongside Rockson.

For a moment Rock felt sure that the knife was intended for *him,* and he stepped to one side. The intruder shouted and ran past him, moving at top speed in the direction of the ruler!

Rock turned swiftly and silently on his heels, realizing that, if he wanted, he could reach the knife arm from behind, and vigorously twist it. But why should he help Panxux? *Oh, hell* . . .

An angry, defiant shout from the intruder's throat changed to screams. His knife hand was forced downward until the weapon clattered to the polywood floor and

144

Rock kicked it away. Only then did he push the man from him, and recognize with whom he had been dealing.

"You!"

It was Broomak, the liberal. Now a mad assassin.

Panxux asked quietly, "Why did you want to do this, Kitra?" He used Broomak's first name.

The knife wielder said in his high, piping voice, "I have come around to Rockson's way of thinking. He's *right!* Life here is all work and no fun!"

The leader said, "You need to be *corrected!* More waste, Kitra, of good manpower thanks to this man from Earth's evil influence!"

"You've been wasting every man and woman on this asteroid," Broomak shouted. "You've been a disaster for Esmerelda, you and your cronies. Every year production *decreases!*"

Panxux spoke to Rock, eyes unwavering: "Stay with him; I'll go to find the guards; they will come take him away. Thanks, I owe you one . . ."

"Good," Rock said, "we'll sit here and talk meanwhile!"

Kitra Broomak stared at the desk where the leader had been sitting. Not a word passed between the failed murderer and the younger man who had doomed him. Soon a guard snapped a pain-bracelet set on "maximum obedience" on the failed killer, and led him away. Rock held the door open and was going to follow the two when the leader's voice called on him to wait.

"Only one more point, Rockson," the man he had saved said, seating himself behind the desk. "I'm aware that I owe you a debt and will find a way to discharge it."

"Just let me have Kimetta to make the instructional videos with."

"I'll see. You realize she's a free woman? She might refuse. I can't order her . . . she's the warden's daughter."

"I know. But she'll come to me." *But would she?*

145

Chapter Twenty-four

He had the 3-D video cameras all set up and ready, and Rock expected Kimetta to show up by midnight. But no go! Just as Rock was shucking his one-piece suit, figuring something had gone wrong, he heard a soft voice calling from the slightly open door. "Hi honey."

He nearly fell back in astonishment upon opening it. Not only was he looking at Kimetta, but she was naked except for some sparkle highlights on random spots — or was it Kimetta's clone, Ronette, without the mask? In any case, she was standing in front of him. She said she *really was* Kimetta, the girl who had helped shanghai him and then had saved him by giving him the Zrano's mother's picture-medallion. He asked her in; she came in.

"It's good to see you," he said, "But you're *Ronette.*"

She blinked twice and sagged, "How did you know?"

"The real Kimetta, well . . . I'll explain to her when she gets here — now go get her. Go on! Get out, honey, and send Kimetta here!"

"I'll leave, but —"

He kissed her. "Maybe some other time." He patted her bare fanny hard and sent her off — not without some regrets.

A short time later a fully clothed, angry Kimetta was at the door when he opened it. "Well, Mr. Perfect, Mr. Privilege," Kimetta said, her blue eyes glaring, "I came here only to tell you off! You sent for me, did you? You want me to make your damned porn movie huh!! Well,

I'm not—"

He smiled. "You're acting just like your old self—the real *Kim,* not Kimetta—Kim is a woman who I dream about—I *hoped* you would act that way. *Now* come in! I have something to discuss."

He pulled the perplexed-looking Kimetta in and shut the door. This idea of his was going to be hard to explain!

"Huh?" she said. "What?"

"Come inside, that's why I asked for you; not for sex—I need some explanations. You brought me here, now *help* me, please.

She did come in, saying, "OK, I *owe* you that."

"What the hell did you do it for, *all* of it! Why hurt me, then *help* me?"

She was thoughtful and calm after he asked that. She sat on the bed and stared into space a while. He almost expected her to take out a square of audi-writing and flick on music. But all she said was "I don't know."

"I think I *do* know, honey," Rock said. "I think all *reality* changed! I think you were compelled to do it all! Yes—don't tell me you don't feel like that happened. Don't you have weird dreams? Dreams of being someone else?"

"No . . . wait! Yes." She smiled. "I dream I'm the president's daughter in a place called America! That I really do love you. Yes Rock, I do dream! Those dreams are why I helped you, even if in *this* reality I'm supposed to hurt you!"

"That's crazy, but I know you're right. I'm dreaming, *now.*"

She nodded. "Yes. In any case," she said, "Panxux informed me that he was desirous of sparing your life and wouldn't consider otherwise unless you violated some other rules or were guilty of treason by not working well on your video-sex tape plan. He favorably mentioned your plan to make the videos to teach your ways of sex pleasure, to increase work productivity. So

I'm to be your co-star! Please, all this talk about dreams and reality hurts my head!"

Rock declined her invitation to begin filming sex instructions. Instead, he sat next to her and said, "I think you're right, like I am, about reality being wrong. I had dreams—that I was someone called the Doomsday Warrior. That I was—trapped in a box, suffocating, dreaming about this place, this world. Kimetta, *Esmerelda isn't real!* Do you believe me, Kimetta?" His mismatched eyes held her. "Say you do!"

"I do."

"Then we've got to escape!"

"How can one escape a dream? Let's just have fun dreaming!" She started to strip off her clothes. "Please, let's have sex! I'm—I'm *scared* of this *talk!* What can we do about wrong realities?"

"I don't *know!* Put—put on your clothes. Let's get going. Can you use your pull to have the guard remove my pain bracelet—to get us at least on the way to the spaceport?"

"Yes . . . I am A-1, and a citizen. I am trusted. I am the warden's daughter. But, how will that—"

"I have the crazy idea," Rockson said, buckling his belt, "that if we escape this asteroid, we escape the dream! And we—I—wake up!"

"I know I was part of this conversation," Kimetta said, "but now, none of this makes the slightest sense to me!"

"It will. Let's go!"

Chapter Twenty-five

They left the arena area in a rocket-car. Rock sighed in relief as his pain-bracelet was taken off by a guard. In a short while Rockson heard sirens, saw police vehicles swooping down. "The radio; put on the police scanner," Rock said.

In a moment they learned that the police weren't after them—there was a rebellion going on. It had started as a general strike, and spread on the news of Kitra Broomak's "attempted correction." Broomak had been rescued by rebels. The radio report blamed "the antiphilosophy of the Earthman, Niles Rockson" for starting the trouble. He was called an "evil dreamer."

Rock said, "Shit is hitting the fan!"

"Yes, everybody suddenly wants to be a rebel, like you," Kimetta smiled, kissing his cheek. "It was bound to happen."

"I can't believe that," Rock said. "Esmerelda was in existence for a long time before I came along, and nobody ever acted up before, I'm told. At least not *en masse!* There's got to be more to it than reaction to what I did."

"There is!" Kimetta said. "Don't you see? We know it's just a dream, so the dream is falling apart! We're doing it!"

Rock nodded. "Not everybody has flipped out because of my philosophy! I'm sure of that!"

Just then their car automatically braked as a mob ran across their path, shouting that they were *free!* Shouting: "Rock, Rockson, Rock, Rockson! Rock, Rockson!" A light pole vanished, a building rocked and faded away into nothingness.

149

"This asteroid is finished," Kimetta said, "I think it will fade away soon! It's not real. It's—my dream, or *your* dream, but it's just the stuff dreams are made of— let's get away before we fade too! Unless what's happening is put under control very quickly, somehow. You wanted to escape, and now it's time to do so. Please, I don't want to—to evaporate."

Once the crowd passed they roared on toward the spaceport. Half a dozen men in one-piece gladiator outfits were running toward them almost as soon as Rock opened a door of the car, which he halted near the ten-story-tall, gleaming rocket ship called *Earth-Mother*.

"We're free, we're on our own," they shouted. "No more games."

The men crowded around him, recognizing the Earthman.

"We owe it all to you, Rockson," one man said enthusiastically. "You're the one who got us free, aren't you, Rock Rockson!"

"Yes, that's right, I guess. Now if you'd let me and Kimetta pass . . ."

The men didn't. They were a solid wall of glee.

"The rebel guards told us that there will be a celebration on account of you, that we're going to be free from now on, and first we'll have fun!"

One man, who'd been holding himself away from the others, said grimly, "As soon as the celebration is over, they'll catch us again, I'm afraid. Then—," he drew a finger across his throat, "no more freedom."

"At least we damn well are going to get what fun we can, for as long as we can," one of the other men retorted. He was shaking Rock's hand. "What's with you? You are our hero, but you look like you just bit into a sour lemna melon. Why?"

"Because," Rock said to the man, "You aren't *real!* I'm *Ted* Rockson, and this is Kim, President Langford's daughter. We are real, and *you're* not!" He pushed a hand *through* the fading man. "Quick, Kim, up the rocket's staircase," he shouted.

But Kimetta was fading too. Her voice, faint and echoing, said, "Good-bye my love, good luck. *I'm a dream too!*"

Rock reached for her, and his hands clutched just air. She was gone. With a lump in his throat and adrenaline in his heart, he turned and started climbing up into the planetary patrol, high-boost, single-seater fighter rocket. *It* seemed real enough! He slammed the airlock, and pressed the emergency boost button.

Chapter Twenty-six

The twin-seat rocket took off in the emergency take-off mode, with all engines firing. Almost immediately, Rockson was crushed back into the brown leatherette cushioning. The G-force was like being hit in the stomach with a baseball bat. And as the super-powerful rocket ship kept rising from the surface, the weight of his body quadrupled and then quadrupled again. Rock was soon near to blacking out, almost unable to draw a breath. He watched the meters before his blurred vision spin around like pinwheels. Klaxons and buzzers were sounding, denoting the strain on the rocket's life-support systems. Soon, the craft would disintegrate!

"Have . . . to . . . cut engines," he thought, and reached for the cut-off lever — or at least what he thought was that lever.

His hand barely cleared the couch, and then fell back. The acceleration was too great to move even an *inch*. He'd just have to hope he'd run out of fuel before he died.

In the rear-mirror viewer above the shaking, smoking control panel, he watched Esmerelda become a marble and then a dot, and then wink out. Nothing but stars, unfamiliar patterns of stars, were out there. The meter, the one that counted off millions of miles traveled (the other meters changed too fast to read) indicated that he was already ten million miles out from the prison-world. The fuel meter read half gone. And so was he.

Rockson couldn't breathe. Even his eyeballs hurt. They felt like lead ball bearings, boring back down into his brain. His vision narrowed, reddened.

"Have to do it," he mumbled, and even that mumble gurgled back into his throat, his saliva choking him.

Steeling his mighty-thewed legs, he gave it one more try, attempting this time to *drop-kick* the control lever. And with one mighty double thrust, his toe just touched the lever — enough to cut power, part way. The invisible pair of elephants on his chest became just a pair of donkeys. He was now able to reach up with his hand and pull the lever to the completely off position.

Suddenly there was total silence, total lack of the teeth-grinding vibration. All the klaxons and emergency buzzers kept ringing for a moment, and then they too cut off. Automatic systems must have begun repairing the damage he had done.

Rock hadn't strapped in, and now, when he craned his neck up to see the array of dials, he floated weightless off the couch. He breathed easily, moved freely.

He twisted in the air, like a trapeze artist. He felt positively giddy due to the lack of oxygen all those minutes he had been accelerating. He checked the dials, hoping to find some indication of his course. He was no astronavigator, but as near as he could figure it, he was set on a course for the Earth's planetary system. Evidently this baby had been programmed for its return trip before he'd boarded. Thank God for that. He'd have to coast most of the way, and then avoid scan-radar back at Earth.

He was exhausted. There was nothing to do for several hours now. He decided to get back down on the couch, strap down, and get some shut-eye.

But when he twisted in midair and started toward the couch, he drew in a sharp, icy breath of air — for he was *already* on the couch! Rockson saw his own body lying there!

Was he dead?

Fear as icy as a frozen icepick jerked into his heart, but he tried to look more carefully. Something was different. There was something wrong with this picture of himself! His body, below his face, was under some sort of covering — a sparkly blanket? No, a metallic chamber. He was seeing not the couch but some sort of iron lung-like capsule. His gaunt, dead face was staring up at him through the ugly metallic capsule's face plate, his eyes open and staring in death, his mouth frozen in the last breath. Then he saw the boulder that had fallen and smashed the — the *what?*

The dream machine. He was inside something called the dream machine. And the machine was not in a spacecraft, but rather in some sort of huge, dark cave.

He just floated there, trying to control himself, trying to keep his mind away from total freak-out. He was on the brink of total screaming insanity, but he controlled, controlled. And Rockson tried to think logically — if a ghost can think, that is.

"I can think," he thought, "therefore I am real. A real *ghost?* Let's be reasonable. If I died, and I'm a ghost floating out of my own body, why the hell is my body in a capsule? Where is the spaceship? Conclusion: You might *not* be dead . . ."

His pounding heart slowed to a mere marathon-race rate. He spun his arm so that his floating body twisted about, drawing his horrified eyes up and away from his own dead frozen stare. The ghost Rockson looked around. It was a dark, huge cave, lit by a few emergency cannister lights. Under him was a stone tile floor scattered with broken pieces of equipment, some bloodstains . . . and other bodies of small men in red tunics, some holding sharp aluminum-looking cylinders — guns? — in their decaying hands.

Where the hell was this? This was something from a dream!

There were ethereal whispers now all around him. Rockson had visitors:

"Where are you?" he called. And *they* floated toward him — other ghosts. Floating about him, smiling, mocking.

A pale, semitransparent, naked Kimetta shook her finger at him. "You shouldn't . . . be here," she whispered like a hiss on the dark wind, as she floated along-side him.

"Where *is* here?" he shouted back, but his voice too was like a ghostly ice-whisper.

She just laughed and faded away.

Then Dovine's fat form drifted past. Dovine was laughing like the ghost of Christmas present in the Dickens novel. And then came Kimetta's father, chewing on grapes and wearing his laurel-leaf crown. The images, all as ghostly as his own airborne body, floated all around him, swirling out at him and laughing.

"Where am I?" he shouted again. "Tell me where I am!"

And this time Kimetta, Dovine, Warden Langdon, Ronette, all of them said in unison, "In a dream, Rockson. You're in a dream, in a dream, in a dream."

"Come back to us," Kimetta's ghostly voice pleaded. "Stay here, in reality. You don't want to be *dead* do you?"

And then Rockson remembered. This *cave* wasn't the dream. Esmerelda, and all those on that hateful asteroid, were the dream. "NO!" Rockson shouted. "I am not dreaming NOW. I won't come back."

Masked Ronette placed an ethereal kiss on his non-face. "What is dreaming?" she asked. "How do you know what is dreaming and what is real?"

"I know!" Rockson shouted, and they all faded away — screaming. He was alone again. Alone, and once more staring down at his body.

"I'm not dead," he whispered, "not dead . . . yet."

"Save yourself," Kimetta's voice whispered from the darkness. "Save yourself."

"Save myself?" How could he? — YES! He managed to think *heavy* and his ghost body gained weight. Eventually ghost Rockson stood on the floor. He leaned over the capsule, holding down sheer terror. He looked inside the face plate. The Rockson inside was *not* dead. He was breathing with difficulty. He looked emaciated, near death. The capsule was dented, cracked at chest level; a

155

large rock must have fallen from the cavern ceiling and smashed it, damaged it. Somehow Rockson the ghost knew that these capsules had life-support systems, and that this one's system had been damaged by the falling rocks that now littered the floor near the capsule. That's what had happened to the man — to the dreamer Rockson inside the capsule! He's hurt.

"Maybe . . . so now what? What do I do?"

The ethereal-wind voice of Kimetta came again: "What would you do if it was somebody *else* in there?"

"Open the capsule. Open the capsule — can a ghost do these things," he wondered. He touched his blue-white fingers to the latches and felt the metal, and he found that, ghost or not, he could exert some pressure on the latches. Better than that, he felt superstrong. He merely thought to unlatch the snaps and they came up, spraying hot, dry air out of the capsule. He reached in and lifted the body — his own body — up in his arms. "Oh my God," he said, "what now?" He shook the sleeping Rockson.

"Wake up," he said. "Please — wake up, so that I can wake up too!" Nothing. It was light, like a thin and dry rag doll, but it was still warm and breathing shallowly. Sobbing in confusion and fear, Rockson the ghost carried Rockson the nearly dead man over to a table, and placed him on top.

"What now?" he addressed the lingering ghosts above.

"What would you do," whispered an ethereal Kimetta from the darkness, "if it was somebody else?"

"I KNOW!" he shouted. And the ghost Rockson immediately started to give himself, the dying Rockson, a careful *examination*. The wound in his chest looked bad. The ghost Rockson ripped apart the man's tunic, revealing his bare and bloody chest. He gasped — if ghosts can gasp. It sounded faint, hollow.

The man's ribs, *his* ribs, were actually caved in. His ribs were broken, bloody ribbons — not bones. SO WHAT? He couldn't do anything about that now. He was no surgeon.

156

"Just keep him breathing. Someone is coming," whispered dream Kimetta.

It seemed hopeless but he put his mouth to his own other mouth, and began CPR. In and out. In and out.

The other Rockson responded after a time, coughing out blood and bits of bone. Choking but strong breaths began to come more steadily.

Ghost Rockson felt relieved. For a moment he felt dizzy. Can ghosts feel dizzy? It was as if . . . as if . . . *yes!* He was actually getting thinner, paler. He realized that he was fading away. He was becoming some sort of spiral in the air, a spiral of pure energy. Life energy. The man on the table breathed more easily, each breath stronger than the last. With the man Rockson's every breath drawing in life energy, the ghost Rockson was losing his being. The ghost Rockson was being dragged into that now-breathing blue-white body. Into pain.

"Help!" he yelled. "No! I don't want to—I don't want to feel that man's pain! It's better to be a ghost! NO! I don't want to . . ."

But it was no use. He was spinning, turning on a shiny silver cord, like bathwater going down a drain. He was slowly but surely being sucked into that body.

Pain! Oh Agony; awful excruciating pain at every breath. And noises, huge thundering blasts. The cave wall was shaking.

And a sharp light to the left as rock wall fell away. Figures clambered through the blasted-in opening.

"Rockson! Get Rockson out of the capsule! There may still be a chance," someone ordered. Flashlight beams cut through the darkness and fell on the man lying on the table. "For the love of God!" someone exclaimed. "He's gotten himself out of the capsule!"

A familiar huge, hairy shape loomed over him in the blinding light of a flashbeam. "Rockson! He's hurt! Call surgeon!"

Archer! It was Archer!

Rock tried to smile, to focus his eyes. He could

157

recognize the voice, smell the man looking at him with such pity. Archer had made it back!

Other hands, small, cold hands, touched and probed him. More pain. A small, faint voice, not meant for him to hear, whispered, "He's in bad shape. We have to perform surgery immediately. Get him lots of whole blood. There's surgical equipment in the back of the cave. Get the gas! I'll perform the operation myself! Here, Archer. While I get the stuff, shoot this into his arm."

And with those words he felt the prick in his arm. The pain eased. Rockson felt only a dark, pleasant oblivion.

Hours later, after stripping off the surgical mask, the Techno-survivor surgeon said to Archer, "I've done all I can. He's still breathing, but I'm not sure I took care of all the internal damage. These mutant-types heal well. Any normal man would have died from those wounds. So I think he'll live. But I'm worried about his brain—all that oxygen deprivation. I don't know if he'll ever come out of his coma."

"He's alive!" Archer insisted.

"We could bring him to Century City. But"—Zydeco looked down at the floor—"brain damage is—irreversible. . . ."

"No! I no believe that!" Archer cried, clutching the man's lapels and lifting the frightened Zydeco off the floor.

And then Archer gasped and let go. Archer's hat flew off and, as the Techno-survivor backed away, Archer started to scream and roar like a bear. There was a blue light shining from out of his head! As they all watched in awe, Archer's crystal-implanted skull glowed. Each of the multifaceted crystals imbedded in his head started glowing.

"What the hell?" Zydeco said. "Archer, are you all right?"

158

"Shhh," Archer said. "I'm getting a message through my crystals! The implanted crystals in my head have been quiet for years!"

"Message?" Zydeco was too amazed to comment on Archer's sudden eloquence.

"From—the Glowers. Now, please, keep quiet!" Archer's veins pulsed, and he moaned and nodded once in a while. Finally the light in the crystals in his head died out.

"What happened?"

"The Glowers gave me instructions to take Rockson someplace much closer than Century City. They say they will try to revive him. Three hundred thirty-one miles. Get me a map, before I forget. My brain hurts," Archer said. "I don't like talking so fast!"

Once he plotted out the way on the map, Archer became his old staring, inarticulate self again.

Quickly Zydeco and Archer arranged a stretcher to carry Rockson out. They placed him in the armored personnel carrier that they had stolen to break out of Zhabnovtown—and, wheels spinning, headed off toward the Glower encampment.

Chapter Twenty-seven

The journey was swift and Archer's directions kept them on course. But when the APC and the other commandeered Sov vehicles arrived at the spot where they expected to find the Glowers, there was no settlement there. "Could we have gotten the directions wrong?" Zydeco worried aloud.

"No!" Archer said, "I tell it right!"

Suddenly there was a humming. No, it was more like the wash sound of electrical currents in the air. Heads swiveled. Binocs were raised, scanning the rocky horizon. Zydeco saw it first: "THERE!" he gasped. "THREE of them."

"Of what?" scientist Myra Flourite asked, focusing in on the same direction.

"I don't know, honestly!" Zydeco gasped. "Three ships. God, they look like old pirate galleons; masts and sails and . . ."

"But there's no *water*," the white-smocked little surgeon exclaimed. "God, I see them, too. They're coming fast! Must be sixty miles an hour. God, they're not on wheels, the three galleons are floating over the surface of the sands!"

The strange ships weren't the half of it. Huge, blue, glowing creatures manned the great sails' ropes, steering the crafts with giant ships' wheels, too. "Monsters!" Zydeco gasped. "Assume defensive positions!" Zydeco called out. The hot-ray men flattened out behind several boulders. Archer hit his forehead with a meaty left palm. "NO SHOOT! Yes, I remember," he said, scratching his flickering, crystal-laden head. "I was on such ship many years ago. No, don't shoot!

160

They are friend!" shouted the not-so-gentle giant. "THEY'RE GLOWERS!"

The ships slid alongside them as they stood in a line of greeting. The mental words came out of a creature of glowing blue brilliance who leaned over. "ARCHER AND THE EIGHT CLOSEST TO HIM, CLIMB UP THE NETS WE THROW DOWN; GET ON BOARD. WE'LL SEND A SLING DOWN FOR THE STRETCHER. DO NOT TOUCH US OR YOU WILL SURELY DIE. THE REST OF YOU WILL RETURN TO REPAIR YOUR HOME."

The big mountain man carried the stretcher containing Rockson over and put it in the lift. Once it was moving up, they all clambered up the soft, warm, plasticlike nets. The deck was awash with flickering blue energy. Everyone's hair stood on end.

Up close now, the Techno-survivors were terrified. The things that had invited them on board stood in a phalanx, staring at them with saucer-shaped, green-yellow eyes. Zydeco and the other Techno-men huddled behind the massive frame of Archer. "You didn't say the Glowers *looked like this!*" Zydeco exclaimed. "Are they human?"

And before Archer could answer, the lead Glower's mind came into all of their minds at the same time. "WE LOOK SO STRANGE BECAUSE OUR ORGANS ARE OUTSIDE OUR SKINS, HELD BY CARTILAGE. WE ARE HELD TOGETHER BY ENERGIES OF THE MIND. THINK OF YOUR OWN BODIES TURNED INSIDE OUT. YOU WOULD LOOK MUCH LIKE WE DO. EXCEPT, OF COURSE, YOU WOULD DIE THAT WAY. BUT YES, WE ARE . . . OF HUMAN ORIGIN."

That answer just seemed to make the Techno-survivors more frightened. So the leader of this band of Glowers sent a burst of mathematical models into the Techno-survivors' minds, so that they might understand the nature of being a Glower more quickly in their own parlance. To Archer, of course, the model the Glower leader sent was much simpler, reminding

Archer that the Glowers were the next step in evolution of mankind beyond the Rockson stage; that their evolution had been pushed forward—perhaps on another track entirely—by radiation; that they were the immortal children of the astronauts whose space station had been bathed in the rays of the nuclear war below them a hundred years earlier; that they were *brothers*, and *Americans*.

That eased minds only *somewhat*. Archer and Zydeco, with the rest of their party huddling behind them, faced the apparent leader, who communicated: "INTRODUCING YOUR MEMBERS IS NOT NECESSARY, WE SCAN YOUR MINDS. I AM THE TURQUOISE SPECTRUM. WE HAVE MET BEFORE, ARCHER, DO YOU REMEMBER?"

Archer nodded. He couldn't tell this "man" from the others physically, but his radiant power was familiar. Answering an unvoiced question from one of the Techno-survivors, the Glower leader spoke in all their minds:

"WE CALLED YOU TO THE NEAREST PLACE OUR SHIPS WOULD BE ABLE TO SAIL. OUR VILLAGE IS MANY MILES DISTANT, FAR OUT IN THE DESERT. WE WILL REACH IT IN A MATTER OF THREE AND A HALF OF YOUR HOURS. ROCKSON WILL NOT DIE IF WE REACH THE MEDICINE IN TIME."

"Why didn't you bring it?" Zydeco asked in a shaky voice.

"THE MEDICINE IS THE *PLACE*, NOT SOME *DRINK*," Turquoise Spectrum responded immediately to the thought. "ONLY THE GREAT ENERGY OF THE AREA WE LIVE IN, AND ITS ANCIENT MEDICINE WHEEL, CAN EFFECT A CURE."

Even as he spoke in their minds the great ships turned into the wind. Their sails shifted position under the guidance of the strange, inside-out beings that handled the guide ropes. The sails caught the wind (or the sunlight), and the ship slowly started to move in the direction from which it had come.

The other two ships followed. Zydeco's thought: "Why *three* ships?" He was immediately responded to. "THOSE ARE GUNSHIPS. THEY CARRY . . ." There was a pause, as if there were no equivalent words. Finally the Glower leader's thought continued. "THEY CARRY WEAPONS UNDREAMT OF EVEN IN YOUR WILDEST IMAGININGS. THERE ARE THINGS IN THE DESERT BETWEEN HERE AND WHERE WE INHABIT. THE ESCORT SHIPS KEEP US SAFE FROM INTRUDERS — INTERDIMENSIONAL BEINGS LET INTO THIS WORLD'S TIME-SPACE BY THE POWER OF THE NUCLEAR BLASTS LONG AGO. THESE THINGS DO NOT RESPOND TO REGULAR DEFENSES. YOU WILL SEE."

About an hour into the trip, something like an alarm went off. As Zydeco, Archer, and the others watched in awe, the two gunships moved ahead of their "hospital" ship, where Rockson still floated over the deck in "medical stasis."

"THEY ARE COMING," the thought came.

"What?" Archer said aloud.

"SHHHH," Turquoise Spectrum said in his mind. "WATCH."

The desert wavered and flickered, as if it were bending, as if reality itself were bending. Then a thing — glowing like the glowers, only a sickly green — jutted out of the sand and tried to take a bite of the prow of the first gunship! The thing had three rows of teeth and must have been fifty feet wide. Only God knew how long. The thing was sort of like a *worm*, but with huge furled wings, with talons set all along their leading edges. Part seagull, part alligator, part earthworm!

As they all shrank back in horror, expecting the gunship to be devoured, the ship and its partner fired strange, rippling red rays at the thing's many-eyed head. The thing's teeth locked onto the hull, bending some of the forward plates of the ship's prow. And then the thing screamed as the red rays hit an eye. It was a weird, other-dimensional scream that shuddered through the spine of each and every human who was watching. It chilled to the bone and deeper. It must have been a square hit, because the thing rose up out of the desert sea and sank beneath the sandy waves.

Zydeco and the others had scarcely caught their breaths when a sight met their eyes that made what they had just witnessed seem a kiddie's tale told in the nursery. The three ships shuddered with the force of some terrible disturbances beneath the dunes. Then the things came bursting out of the sands—a veritable armada of horrid, glowing worm-bird-reptile creatures, with jaws the size of tanks. There must have been twenty or more of the neon nightmares leaping in and out of the dunes like flying fish. When they screamed, the green-gray platelets—scales around their worm necks—ruffled. Red flesh rattles slid out between their scales, making a horrible din. Strangest of all, the worm things seemed to *pulse* in and out of existence, as if a strobe light played on them.

They moved fast. One would be in one place and wink out. The next sighting, it would have moved to a completely different area. The two gunships flanked the hospital ship, sending out their own kind of wobbly, red death rays from very odd weapons. Zydeco, Archer, and the other humans could see devices resembling TV "rabbit ear" antennas rising from the decks of the gunships. *Nyerp*ing arcs of red and blue light were discharged into the air. The Glower leader, Turquoise Spectrum, tried to explain telepathically that the weapons were somehow linked into the creatures' strobe-rhythms, the kill rays winking in and out of existence *with* the monsters. Or, to be more technical, *following* them into whatever dimension they tried to escape to. They were called strobe-pulsers. And they had better work!

The gun crews had all they could do to direct the weapons at the creatures and time them to the exact pulse of the creature's dimension-jumping pulse, before they devoured the ships and their crews. If the shots were mistimed, the weapon and the creature would be out of sync. They weren't mistimed!

The worm screams and thunderous worm rattles were deafening. That and the constant barrage of the weapons made the humans hold their ears.

The hospital ship was tossed from side to side by the writhing bodies of the dying thunder-worms. The gunships at all times sailed to protect the hospital ship. Rockson's body, floating in its energy cocoon, swayed back and forth with the ship. He was totally unconcerned about the danger, about his earthly existence. Archer stayed right with him. The worst part about watching was the utter helplessness of Archer, Zydeco, and the Techno-survivors. No weapon they had could possibly touch these monsters from a sandy hell!

Each gunship was kept busy battling with these winking, blinking monsters, when suddenly a huge, flying worm broke through the defenses and leaped over the deck of the hospital ship, just missing Rockson's stasis cocoon. Random Vector, one of the bravest of the Techno-survivors, saw his chance for action. He ran straight to the end of the deck and jumped into the sandy sea. The worm's jaws poised over Rockson, but that immense, horrible monster was diverted by the jumper. It chased after him, *dove* after him. Random Vector's diversionary action not only saved Rockson, but the entire hospital ship, from certain destruction. As the worm thing *ate* the heroic man, they heard Random Vector's mind waves: "I, RANDOM VECTOR, AM NO MORE. GOOD-BYE FRIENDS. MY BODY IS NO LONGER, BUT THE PART OF ME THAT IS THE WHOLE STAYS WITH YOU."

The gunships continued the battle against the worms. Archer, Zydeco, and the other Techno-survivors watched in horror, their hair standing on end, this jagged nightmare of constant weapons' sounds, pulsing screams, and rattles. The hospital ship tossed so much from side to side that they had all they could do to hold on. Archer could feel his stomach beginning to heave — seasickness on the desert!

Then, suddenly, it was over. The last of the attacking worms had been hit, and was screaming the awful scream of defeat. Then it winked out of existence. There were no other Glower or human casualties. All that was left was total silence and the distinct smell of ozone burning their nostrils, and the memory of Random Vector's ultimate sacrifice for his fellow men.

"THE DANGER IS OVER," said Turquoise, "FOR NOW." They sailed on.

When they reached the area between the dozen geodesic domes, blue lit from inside, the sand ships slowed and many Glowers came running out with huge poles. The poles, Archer knew, would steady the ships, so they would not lean over on their sides, for once the sails went down, the ships were no longer capable of floating.

When the poles were in place and their great sail ship creaked down into their cradling arms, they all climbed down the ropes and then the Glowers lowered the cocoon that contained their desperately sick friend, Rockson.

The stretcher bearers took him from the stasis cocoon and carried him, as directed, into the largest of the domes.

As they were led inside the dome, the mountain man and his companions were again admonished not to touch their hosts. The bearers were ordered to lay Rockson on a sand painting of lightning bolts near the center of the twenty-foot-wide dome's floor. Then they were told by Turquoise to sit on small rocks that were set in a circle near the walls of the structure. Turquoise and four other Glowers, as they came into the lodge, each picked up a circular shields about two feet wide. As they too sat, they placed the small, intricately decorated shields before them, so their bodies were mostly covered by them.

That made them look less weird to Archer. The shield hid all those pumping organs that made Archer feel so uncomfortable when he looked at them.

"BUT THAT IS NOT THE PURPOSE OF THE SHIELDS," Turquoise Spectrum said in his mind. "EACH SHIELD PATTERN SHOWS THE ACCOMPLISHMENTS OF OUR BEING, WHERE WE ARE ON THE PATH TO COMPLETION." He sent Archer a burst of symbols. Archer grasped, someplace deep inside him, a pure *understanding:* an understanding that each person is a wheel, as the universe is a wheel; an understanding that we are born with only one part of the great wheel's nature . . . male or female, active or passive, yang or yin, we are incomplete. In order to be whole, to pass on to a higher plane of existence, to progress toward its ultimate destiny—union and completion in the universe—a being must travel around that wheel, integrating all the energies of the mind and body.

Archer groaned, holding his head. Never had he had such a profound thought.

"WE HAVE BEEN ON THIS LAND A LONG TIME, AND HAVE COME TO FEEL RELATED TO THE INDIANS WHO ONCE LIVED IN THIS LAND," Turquoise Spectrum said, in Archer's mind. "THEIR SPIRITS—THEIR MOST POWERFUL MEDICINE MEN—STILL ROAM HERE. WE HAVE INTEGRATED THOSE SPIRITS INTO OURS, AND HAVE LEARNED MUCH."

"That is all well and good," Zydeco's voice flared up, "but how can this discussion help our gravely ill friend, who, as we discuss these abstract things, breathes with great labor? Can you not do something?"

"WE HAVE ALREADY ANALYZED THE PROBLEM. THERE IS NO PHYSICAL MEDICINE THAT CAN CURE HIM, OR IT WOULD HAVE ALREADY BEEN DONE. ROCKSON HAS BEEN REMOVED FROM THIS REALITY. HIS DREAM WAS SO REAL

TO HIM THAT . . ." Turquoise Spectrum looked up at the pale sun which could be seen right through the dome's transparent material, obscured by fast-moving bands of red clouds. "ROCKSON IS NOT REALLY HERE. HIS CELLS THEMSELVES ARE TIED TO ANOTHER UNIVERSE THAT COLLAPSED WHEN THE DREAM MACHINE BROKE. AND HE IS NO MORE."

"Then there is no hope? Are we going to just sit and talk philosophy and watch him die?" Zydeco was much alarmed.

"NO. WE WILL DO THE MEDICINE WHEEL PRACTICE OF REINTEGRATION. WITH THE CYCLE OF THE GREAT MEDICINE WHEEL, THERE IS A CHANGE. YOU ALL MUST PARTICIPATE. IF IT WERE JUST ROCKSON AND WE GLOWERS, WE COULD NOT RELATE TO HIM ENOUGH. ARCHER, ESPECIALLY, IS TUNED TO THE WAY ROCKSON USED TO BE. AND YOU SEVEN SMALL MEN, YOU TECHNO-SURVIVORS, HAVE GREAT MIND POWER, THOUGH YOUR BODIES ARE FRAIL. IN ORDER TO REINTEGRATE ROCKSON, IF IT CAN BE DONE, ALL OF US COMBINED MUST DO THE MEDICINE WHEEL RITUAL. TRY TO BRING HIM BACK INTO FOCUS IN THIS UNIVERSE.

"I SENSE YOUR IMPATIENCE, HUMANS," Turquoise Spectrum said. "YOU FEAR FOR THE LIFE OF YOUR DYING FRIEND, AND THAT IS GOOD. BUT WE MUST BECOME WHOLE SO THAT WE CAN GIVE ROCKSON THAT WHOLENESS. HE WILL BE THE RECIPIENT OF THAT WHOLENESS, AND THUS, PERHAPS, RESTORED."

The thought transference went on: "THE GREATEST SECRET OF THE INDIANS WAS THE MEDICINE WHEEL. BUT IT WAS AN OPEN SECRET. THERE WERE SIX MILLION MEDICINE WHEELS IN THE AMERICAS. SETTLERS FOUND THEM EVERYWHERE, FROM MAINE TO CALIFORNIA. REMNANTS EXIST TODAY, BUT MOSTLY IN THE DESERTS. FOR IN EVERY WESTERN FOREST, IN EVERY WESTERN PLAIN AND PRAIRIE LAND, THERE WERE SUCH CIRCLES. THEY ARE ALIGNED TO THE BRIGHT STARS, SO THE WHITES THOUGHT THE WHEELS HAD SOMETHING TO DO

WITH CALENDARS, OR CROP PLANTING, OR ASTRONOMY.
THAT IS TRUE, BUT IT IS NOT THE HEART OF THE INDIAN
WAY! THAT, THE WHITES DID NOT UNDERSTAND! IT IS
THE WAY OF COMPLETION, THE ROUNDING OF THE CIR-
CLE. EVERY PERSON IS BORN WITH CERTAIN POWERS.
THIS POWER IS THE BEGINNING OF THE WHEEL.

"NOW LET US BEGIN!"

Chapter Twenty-eight

Aside from Rockson, there were twelve in all: Archer, seven Techno-survivors, and four Glowers. They sat in the wide circle, each on a whitewashed medicine rock. Turquoise used his deep oral voice, not his mind voice, to explain to them gently the nature of the medicine wheel. "The Indians that were here before the Europeans had millions of these circles in North America. They recognized that a healing, a reentering the circle of nature, of the universe, was vital to health and sanity. So they gathered at certain times of year to share—wholeness. The men of today, the technical, logical men and women of today, have forgotten this need to interconnect. They have surrendered wholeness to material power. But we have relearned the power way of the original Americans. We Glowers teach you now as the Indians once taught their children.

"There are four great directional powers in the world and thus in this medicine wheel: to the north, where I sit, is wisdom. Wisdom's color is white, like snow. And the medicine animal of the north is the elk. But wisdom needs other things: compassion, otherness, to be complete.

"In the south of the great circle of life, where Archer sits, is the power of innocence and devotion to others: the heart nature. Its color is green. And its animal is the mouse.

"To the east is the eagle. He can see keenly and is cruelly aware—that is science today, and medicine of the technical nature. Its color is golden brown.

"The west is the wolf, which gathers all the information it needs for the brood to survive. The man of the west—such as Rockson—looks inward and outward, but is always the leader of the pack. Its color is red.

"These are the four basic symbols. The in-between directions are represented by the animals called bear, buffalo, hawk, pheasant, otter, beaver, squirrel, deer. They are the little brothers of the primary animals. The shields also have black arrows pointing toward the center or outward. Inward-pointing arrows denote introspection, outward-pointing arrows denote panoramic awareness. Thus, when we see a being's shield, we know his starting point on the great wheel."

Turquoise Spectrum made a sweeping gesture with his right hand and materialized a rawhide shield in front of each of the humans sitting with him. And all of them were amazed. "Look at your symbols now," Turquoise Spectrum said, "and learn about yourselves."

Archer quickly turned his shield. The huge mountain man expected an elk, or something big and strong. He was disappointed. Archer's shield was rather humbling for a big man. It contained a small and very plain green mouse, which was surrounded by tiny arrows pointing inward. "So," he fumed inwardly, "so I am a nearsighted mouse that sees everything nearby well, but doesn't think of other things!" Archer grumbled and shifted uncomfortably, mumbling into his massive tangle of beard. He wanted to have the elk! He wanted to be *large,* not small. He would be *intelligent, sharp.* And instantly, he realized he *could* be those things, *if* he could do as Turquoise instructed. So Archer got very serious.

Surgeon Escadrille turned his shield and bent his head to see that his shield contained the golden brown hawk, brother animal to the eagle of the east. Hawks see both at a distance and closely. His black arrows pointed outward, thus symbolizing his strength of panoramic awareness, most suitable for a scientist or doctor. The hawk, he intuited, symbolized the power of intelligence a doctor needs. He looked around, catching glimpses of other shields, knowing the nature of the others, knowing what he lacked. And he wanted to be complete.

Zydeco studied his own shield, and the shields of all the other Techno-survivors. Except for the surgeon's, they all were identical. Zydeco had in common with his friends the golden brown eagle of the east, the exact opposite of Archer. Eagle people had panoramic awareness but would never feel close to things, be touched by the heart. Zydeco's shield had arrows pointing outward at the borders, indicating, perhaps, a potential for great achievement. He had to admit that the symbols were good summaries of pyschological-philosophical dispositions, at least in the strange Glower terminology. But *how* a symbol could help *cure* someone—well, he was much more than skeptical. Still, he kept an open mind. The Glowers were amazing beings!

Turquoise spoke: "We beings are very disparate in strengths and weaknesses. We have different capacities, different needs. Throw aside skepticism and all vainglory; be of open heart and mind!" Now the Glower leader used his mind force. He thought-spoke to all of them: "THE GREAT WHEEL RITUAL WILL BEGIN. THOUGH YOU WILL FEEL AS IF YOU ARE LOSING YOURSELVES, DO NOT WORRY. YOU WILL REGAIN YOURSELVES, FEELING MUCH RICHER IN POWER. NOW, COME AND WE WILL EXPLORE THE POLLEN PATH AS WE LINK OUR MINDS. LET US BE QUICK. YOUR FRIEND, ROCKSON, HAS BEEN WANING. HE HAS LESS THAN A HALF HOUR. I CAN TELL YOU WITH ASSURANCE THAT HE WILL NOT REVIVE UNLESS WE CAN GIVE HIM THE POWER OF ALL THE SHIELDS! THE MEDICINE WHEEL MUST SPIN!"

Turquoise turned his thought-beam upon Archer, and the mountain man alone heard the admonition: "ARCHER, PULL YOURSELF TOGETHER, STEADY YOUR MIND! YOUR FRIEND NEEDS YOU ABOVE ALL. THIS IS NOT A MATTER

OF PRIDE. THERE ARE NO BETTER AND LESSER SHIELDS! BESIDES, YOU ARE A GREAT WARRIOR. YOUR GREAT GIFT IS THAT YOU ARE IN TOUCH WITH THE PRESENT, THE HERE AND NOW. THIS GROUNDING IS VITAL TO ROCKSON. YOU WILL SEE AND UNDERSTAND MANY THINGS THAT WILL ADD TO YOUR SHIELD. YOU WILL BE THE MOST NECESSARY TO HELP A FRIEND. DO YOU UNDERSTAND?"

Archer nodded. He calmed down, swallowing his hurt pride. But he shot out the words, "Only to save Rock!"

"NOW WE SPIN THE WHEEL. THE GREAT MEDICINE WHEEL!"

They sat for a long time cross-legged, staring at the center, at Rockson. Finally Archer felt woozy. It wasn't the heat, though the sunlight coming into the dome from above was getting very hot. No, it was a strange beam of light caused by the sun rays coming through an opening at the top of the dome, striking Turquoise's mighty shield. The reflection from the shiny white elk shield shot into each of their minds. Archer, the others, felt—light. They were floating off the sand floor, as a matter of fact!

They seemed to rotate—and each of them felt a LOSS. A loss of more than weight. A loss of identity.

Zydeco gasped. He was Archer, and then he wasn't. He didn't know who he was in the circle of twelve. He decided he was a white elk being, the great Turquoise himself, and nearly screamed. The power of his mind! Oh my God, how could he stand it! Zydeco's shield, across the way, instantly received a bolt from Turquoise's all-powerful mind and changed to add the elk symbol. Then Zydeco's consciousness passed to the next body-soul matrix. And the next.

For Archer, the experience was different. First of all, to feel light, being four hundred and ten pounds heavy, was a very odd sensation indeed. And so the flux of his ego

173

loss came by surprise. He was released instantly from his rather defensive mental makeup. Years of holding himself inward and tight were now just — gone! He didn't have to do that now. Archer, as the beam of light hit him from Turquoise's great shield, understood that he was no longer in need of hiding. He understood that he had been always trying to avoid being hurt, that he had a great fear of being made fun of. He groaned. That defensiveness was a prideful thing, a thing that must be laid aside. Then a beam of light shot from Turquoise's great shield to Archer's shield. The mouse now shared the shield with the elk! Arrows turned out. Archer felt a shift of his very essence then, and his vision cleared. He was staring at himself from the other side of the dome.

How could this be? His panic subsided when he realized he was now looking through the calm, clear eyes of the surgeon, and feeling and thinking like the surgeon. And then a beam of light shot from his shield, the surgeon's shield, toward Archer. Archer's shield now also contained a hawk!

And Archer's consciousness again blurred and he became Zydeco; and then he was another being, and another, and another!

The surgeon looked down incredulously at his massive body, his tangled beard. "God, what was this? I am actually Archer. No, think for a second? Hallucination. Has to be." He squeezed his eyes shut, big watery things, and opened them again; still he was Archer. Turquoise said to just let it go. Surgeon Escadrille remembered, and tried. And then there was relief. It was alright to be Archer — and it was over. Now he was himself again — the little body, so frail. He had never felt so frail until he had been Archer for a moment. The surgeon smiled and realized he still felt the strength of the great bearlike man he had been. So he looked at his shield and saw the change. Another pattern had been added to his hawk shield: Archer's inward pointing arrows and green mouse. Escadrille understood a little more of his self nature. And he had more feeling. Yes, that was the word. He was becoming whole, sharing all the directional powers.

The process of interconnection, integration, continued. Each of them in turn exchanged something—weakness for insight, compassion, strength. After a time, they were all done. Finally they were ready to aid Rockson.

The Turquoise Spectrum mind-spoke to them all: "EACH OF US HAS LEARNED. NOW WE ARE READY. WE WILL ACCOMPLISH THIS THING. RESOLVE THAT WE WILL GIVE OUR POWER TO ROCKSON, DRAG HIM OUT OF THAT NETHERWORLD OF HALF-DREAM, HALF-AWAKENING . . . RESOLVE IT, AND LET US BEGIN THE STRUGGLE FOR HIS LIFE! LET US DO IT NOW! CONCENTRATE ALL YOUR POWER UPON HIS SHIELD, SO THAT HE MIGHT RECONNECT TO THIS WORLD, SO THAT HE WILL HAVE THE POWER OF LIFE ENERGY ONCE MORE!"

Chapter Twenty-nine

All were now linked in mind and heart. They all looked with even greater sadness at the prone, shallow-breathing form of their friend Rockson. His shield was dark and empty, like his life force. Just the great blank shield covered him. But being united mind and heart meant that they made up the whole. And as they understood, the whole is greater than the sum of its parts.

Blue electricity filled the air like a great dynamo ready to start. Their power was awesome.

The Glowers now began a low hum, a discordant yet somehow beautiful dirge. Flashes of light as bright as the sun shot from everywhere and nowhere, all around the dome. As they all concentrated their mental energies on Rockson's body and the great blank shield over him, the Glowers' hum became a beautiful song, grew louder. Snaps and crackles of static electricity filled the air. Even Archer's beard was standing on end. The flashes of light intensified, ricocheting, pulsing faster and faster, becoming a vibrating kaleidoscope of swirling colors and shapes.

With a terrific thunderous clap, the dynamic energy shot out in the form of lightning flashes from each of the participant's shields and flowed into Rockson's shield. Rockson's blank rawhide shield became full of moving colors and shapes. Beams of light shot out from the shield to Rockson's body and back — which made the shield grow brighter still, until there was an all-powerful interflow of energy from shield to Rockson to the shield. The shield and Rockson grew in brightness, until they rivaled the sun. Angels sang, demons howled.

Simultaneously, all assembled around the circle started to rise higher, still in a sitting position, hovering in the air. When they had risen approximately a foot off the ground, they started to spin slowly around Rockson. Each mind link to Rockson became clear, represented by a visual light-spoke of the wheel. The wheel began to turn slowly and then faster and faster. It all spun around Rockson. The whole assemblage and Rockson became the spinning medicine wheel! The completion, the beginning.

Suddenly the colors and shapes on Rockson's shield hardened and solidified into a beautiful mosaic. And then the mosaic resolved into Rockson's personality. The brilliance faded, and a red wolf formed on the shield; the inward and outward pointing arrows became manifest. The flashing lights went out in one final burst, and all fell over swooning in their places. The wheel had stopped. The energy had been transferred.

Rockson sat up. "God, where? *Oh,* now I understand! You all helped me," he croaked out. "Thank you."

"Here, drink this," surgeon Escadrille said, handing him a glass of blue liquid.

Rockson drank it and it steadied his tremors. "Thank you."

"Now rest. Sleep first. We will talk later. We all will rest."

Archer yawned and stretched and lay back where he was. He was the first awake, but soon all the Techno-survivors arose, too. They had slept the sleep of the exhausted on their beds of straw that the Glowers had piled into one empty geodesic dome. Rockson had snored as loudly as Archer, to the consternation of the little techno-survivors.

The Glowers—God knew how they did it—produced a large breakfast. There was the smell of bacon, and fried eggs, and toast.

They ate heartily. "Perhaps the Glowers can *materialize* food," Rockson speculated. The Glowers sat communing with each other, without touching of course, off to the side.

Zydeco, as he sipped his mug of coffee, said, "I never

thought about anything except logic and science before. It is a startling revelation to me to experience this . . . other side of life. What would you call it? What happened yesterday?"

"Spiritual?" Rockson said. "Metaphysical? Is that the term? No. I think a better word would be "Warrior power.""

"Yes, that's it. I thought I knew it all," Zydeco said. "And I knew *nothing*. My understanding of life was so shallow—"

Archer put his arm over the little man. "You know now."

They all were rather quiet for the rest of their meal.

The morning light shone through the cracks in the tentlike top of the lodge-dome. It was a morning of beauty; the blue sky peeking in was shot with icy sky crystals, and a red sun glowed magnificently.

The Glower leader opened the door, letting in cold air just as they finished breakfast. "WE MUST BEGIN THE JOURNEY BACK TO CENTURY CITY. THIS LOCATION IS DANGEROUS FOR HUMANS AFTER A SHORT TIME."

When they came outside, Rockson gasped. It had snowed several feet during the night. It was beautiful. The strange trees that surrounded the circular settlement had coatings of ice. "Like a fairy forest," Zydeco said. "Beautiful."

And the geodesic domes too were ice coated, glowing blue from inside. Turquoise spoke in their minds:

"WE CAN'T SAIL THE SANDSHIPS OVER SNOW, BUT THERE IS YET ANOTHER SHIP. IT HAD BEEN COMPLETED JUST BEFORE WE FELT THE DANGER YOU WERE IN, ROCKSON. COME, WE WILL SHOW YOU OUR GREATEST PHYSICAL ACHIEVEMENT—OUR SNOWSHIP."

Rockson had the brief flicker of a thought about the other-dimensional worm creatures they must pass by to get the hell out of this part of the world. "Will the gunships be able to accompany us?" he asked.

"THERE WILL BE NO NEED FOR GUNSHIPS," said the Turquoise Spectrum. "THE INTERWORLD WORMS WILL NOT ATTACK US. THE BEAUTY OF SNOW TRAVEL IS THAT WITH THE SNOW THERE ARE NO BEINGS SUCH AS THAT. SNOW, GENTLE SOFT SNOW—WATER IN SOLID CRYSTAL FORM—SERVES AS A NATURAL BARRIER TO THE NETHERWORLDS. ALL WE NEED IS

178

Rockson, Archer, and Zydeco and the other Techno-survivors all followed Turquoise Spectrum, eagerly trudging down the path that Glower vaporized in the snow before them with a strange bubble-ray wand.

They came eventually to a great geodesic-shaped hangar, situated between two huge natural monuments of stone. The hangar was oval, elongated and large, perhaps a hundred and fifty meters long by a hundred meters wide. It was several stories high and glowed blue from the inside, like some huge cocoon. Shadows moved inside, cast against the eerie interior light. And as the travelers gaped in awe, the unseen hinges moved and doors slid open, revealing the looming shape inside. It was the great snowship, supported on large timbers. The twelve-foot-diameter stabilizer ball was spinning slightly under the center of the craft.

A dozen Glowers were prying the poles out from under the great craft. The roller ball spun faster and faster. Rockson had learned that it was a sort of gyroscope that spun so fast that it reduced the craft's weight in the gravitational field of the planet. The ship above it stabilized and actually hovered above the concrete flooring of the hangar dome. The great prow of the ship, a ship that seemed to made of crystal ice, started to float slowly out the immense doors.

It was like a Spanish galleon, but twice the size, and immensely more beautiful than the sandships.

"BEHOLD THE SNOW-SHIP," Turquoise said proudly in their minds. "IT RIDES HIGH AND FAST. ZYDECO TELLS ME THAT HIS LITTLE PEOPLE WISH TO ACCOMPANY ROCKSON AND ARCHER TO THEIR HOME. THIS ICE-CARVED VESSEL WILL TAKE YOU ALL BACK TO CENTURY CITY WITH ALL GREAT SPEED."

The magnificent, impossible snowship slid its full hundred-meter length out of the hangar. The back of it was shaped to hold rooms, with lights coming out of portholes. "THOSE ARE YOUR COMFORTABLE QUARTERS. THE JOURNEY WILL PERHAPS BE TOO INTERESTING FOR MANY OF YOU TO WISH TO RETIRE, BUT THERE ARE WARM PLACES AND BEDS."

As Rockson watched, the ship seemed to lower itself a bit,

scattering up a spray of snow. The twelve-foot roller ball spun slightly slower under the center of the craft.

Once the craft had totally emerged from its hiding place, the crew on deck dropped the strange, pink, warm nets for them all to scramble up. It would be quite a climb. This baby was *high*.

"Come," Turquoise said proudly, "let us get aboard."

Chapter Thirty

Despite the concern voiced by surgeon Escadrille regarding his recent illness, Rock was the first to try the net. He pushed off Archer's attempt to steady him. "I'm all right." It was a long climb, over sixty feet up to the deck. Rockson made it a race to the great forward jutting bow. He won — although he suspected Archer could have beaten him. Perhaps the gentle mass of mountain man had held back just a little bit. Rockson felt very strong, but he was not foolish enough to think that he had yet full recovered.

Rock watched the others climb aboard, and while the last of the nets were drawn up, heard an electronic hissing sound like a thousand stereo sets getting ready to blast. The whine was loud enough to make them all hold their ears. Rock knew that the "ball of power" that was embedded in the ship's hull made that noise. The gyro-ball beneath the ship raised it still higher over the snow. Then Rockson felt the ship start to turn in the air — to face toward Century City.

Breathing hard in the icy air, with the wind whipping his long black locks streaked with the one band of ultrawhite, Rock watched along with the others in his party as the great sails were slowly raised into place. First rose the canvaslike wind sail, then the other iridescent, strange, thin fabrics made, not for the wind, but for more subtle energies. The star-energy sail was raised second, black and flickering with strange electrical flows. Finally the powerful, yet most ethereal of all the sails — the one that would catch the power of the earth's magnetic field — The *auroral-sail!*

Once the three sails were up and roped into place, the Glower crew-master went to the great wheel, which was like the wheel on an old sailing ship, and untied it. And then the ship, which seemed to be vibrating like an eager racehorse, began to slide forward out of the rocky area and out above the snow-swept terrain.

They quickly gathered speed, to about thirty knots, and in five minutes were sliding past the Glower village, where the two dozen Glowers that remained behind lined up and silently waved good-bye. But though there was no sound, there was such a mental interchange of emotions and farewell cheers that Rock and his friends held their heads in dismay. They were getting migraines by the time the ship sailed by.

Once the ice-crystal snowship had left the Glowers' geodesic domes behind, a snowstorm began in earnest and a leaden sky seemed to lower on them. But the snow swirled by even faster—the wind picking up added to the power of the other sails. They were whipping along like a jet.

Rockson stayed in the bow section as the others wandered about the ship, studying its mechanism with enraptured attention. The technically minded little men were especially interested in how the Glowers steered the thing. Rock stayed at the prow, and so did Archer, but as the ship rocked like a cradle, Archer soon bunked out on a blanket right next to Rockson. The Doomsday Warrior was alone in his thoughts, standing in the very foremost part of the great craft, watching the terrain slide by, a winter wonderland.

Further back on the craft, Rock knew, the swirling snow thrown up by the great ship's passing would cloud the view. But up here it was breathtaking, and more. Up here there was a solitude that let him dream a bit of the alternate-reality Kim that he had left behind on the nonexistent asteroid named Esmerelda. And Kimetta's face seemed to float in front of the ship sometimes, smiling, encouraging, throwing kisses of icy gusts of snow from the other reality, saying, "I am here, I am well, and I will come to you again."

He was both drawn to the vision and wary of it, wondering if it was dangerous to engage such thoughts. Would he slip into the other reality again? No, he knew he wouldn't. He felt solid, substantial, real; and tied to this time-space plane of existence. She would always be in his dreams, but Kinetta didn't belong *here*. Or Rockson *there*. He found himself supplanting her vision with the thought of her lovely counterpart in this reality — Kim Langford, the president's daughter. Her face formed in the snow clouds.

"Yes, my love, I am waiting for you," Kim seemed to say. And then she too was just a swirling mass of snow dust. Rock smiled and watched the rolling snow dunes, and the ship silently glided along, leaning slightly this way and that as the great sails caught the various ethereal currents of energy it used to move.

The snow dunes were *really* piling up. The clearance of the craft from the real ground below stayed the same; that meant that occasionally the prow would hit the dunes and Rock would feel a lurch. But the craft easily cleared all but the highest snow dunes to be glided over. The gentle tug of the crest of one large dune or another bumping the prow created no danger, just a sensation of slowing for a few seconds. The ship, Rockson had been told, could make more than one hundred and thirty knots per hour, but would be run slower until the snow was less deep. It was utterly safe, and pleasant, he was assured. And that was surely true. The journey seemed to Rockson like a pleasant dream that would last for two days.

The clouds broke slightly at sundown, and at twilight Rockson faced a bloodshot sky. Archer stirred and turned to the side, bumping against Rockson's feet. God, it is so beautiful, should I waken him? No, let the gentle giant sleep. He deserved some shut-eye. Archer was more than a friend, he was like a brother. If your brother could be a hairy bear, that is!

Soon the sun display turned to vermilion, and then to black. Night descended, the broken clouds shot with starlight. The sails rippled and caught their gentle light and amplified it, used it. Rockson knew that was happening when the second sail began to hiss. They picked up speed, the bow grabbing at the highest dunes, rocking more ear-

183

nestly. Rock figured they were going about seventy knots, and the wind was so fierce and cold that he shook Archer awake, and they retired to the cabin that had been provided them. The Techno-survivors had their own warmer cabin, but the two humans had an unused cargo space, twenty steps down inside the hull, for their rest. Twin bunks, one larger than the other, made of — Rock touched it and smiled — yes, it smelled like pine and it *was* pine. All the comforts of a bunkhouse out west, on a strange alien vessel.

For a terrifying instant just before he went to sleep, Rockson thought that he heard one of the other-dimensional invader-worms roaring far out in the wilderness. But then he decided it was just his imagination, and the ship rocked him to sleep. . . .

The next day, he was groggy, even though he woke up long after dawn. After making a pit stop at a simple hole-in-the-flooring bathroom, he splashed some water from a basin on his face. Then went up on deck, which was bathed in sunlight. Squinting in the too-bright winter sun, he was then handed some strange wraparound glasses by Archer, who was already sitting on a long plastic bench, eating breakfast with the little people. The Glowers were up on the rigging, or down in the depths of the ship, or at the great steering wheel, tending to their tasks. They didn't eat breakfast. Not this kind of breakfast. Rock sat down and gaped at the repast. "God, where'd they get this pile of scrambled eggs and toast and bacon and—?"

"*Don't* ask," Zydeco said, spooning a piece of bacon carefully into his mouth, "I asked, and it sorta spoiled my appetite."

Rockson nodded, and ate heartily. And then, as he and a burping, farting Archer made their way up to the prow of the craft, stretching and yawning, he *had* to ask.

"Okay Arch, where *do* the Glowers get this food?"

"Reprocessed shit," Archer said, smiling. "Good!"

Rockson squelched down his gagging feeling and nodded. "OK, thanks for the info." He felt as green as Zydeco had looked for a while. But what the hell, he tried to tell himself, all nature is a series of reprocessing steps — fertilizer raises grass, the hay eaten by cattle making their meat, which we turn into food. . . . He thought like that until his stomach stopped quaking.

They continued their smooth, uneventful, beautiful journey toward Century City.

"Boy," he said to Archer, "see those cliffs over there? That's the Outer Buttes — three hundred snowy miles to go! Man, I've never seen snow of this depth in Colorado. Hey Archer, wait till the guys back home see this thing coming. The portal guards, especially old Gabby, will shit in their pants."

"WILL SHOOT AT US?" Archer asked with some concern.

Rockson laughed. "Now, we thought of that! They won't shoot. I will inform Jarrety and the other receiver mutants in C.C. by telepathy that we're coming, once we get within ten miles."

Archer smiled, "Like Glowers?"

"You got it Arch!" He was, of course, referring to telepathic messages that Rockson — a star-mutant — would send to the three other trained star-mutants in the city, messages that would gently tip the city masters off to expect Rockson to arrive soon — in a strange conveyance! Of course, the Glowers could reach the three telepaths in Century City right from here — but Rock had advised them that their loud and strange mind-links would upset the starpaths of C.C. That's what Jarrety and the others were called. No, that wouldn't do. Instead, once the ship was closing on the city's secret location, Rockson would speak softly into their minds, while they slept perhaps. And all would be well. Not that C.C.'s weapons could do much damage to this baby!

As the sun rose higher and higher and rivulets of melting snow began to form in the dunes below them, threatening early floods, they glided over the torn landscape at a speed that was now truly breathtaking.

The Rocky Mountains came out of the mists looking like white monuments, half covering the sky. Rockson, upon seeing Carson Mountain gleaming in the sunlight, felt a tugging at his heart that every member of Century City's population did upon seeing home after a long journey.

Chapter Thirty-one

Through his electro-binocs Rockson scanned the mountainside as the ship glided to a halt a half mile short of the entrance. A thousand or more people, colorfully dressed in winter parkas denoting their job status in the city, were shouting and waving. And there was firing of many-colored flares.

Rockson had managed a solid contact telepathically and all had been apprised of his coming in the great Glower craft. They were welcomed wildly! Turquoise said, "WHILE THE OTHER STAY ABOARD, I WILL GO WITH YOU, ROCKSON, TO ADDRESS THE ASSEMBLY OF THE COUNCIL AND ELDERS OF THE CITY."

Kim *and* Rona were there to greet Rock. The women each hugged him. Then Rockson — and with some greater difficulty, Archer — was carried aloft back to the city in triumph. Each woman had whispered in Rock's inflamed ears that they had settled their jealous differences while he was away, and that they would see him later in his bedchamber!

People made a wide swath for Turquoise, who walked solemnly and steadily onto the wide entrance ramp. "Say something Rock," someone yelled.

"It's *so* good to be back home!" Rock said, and they all cheered. "But there are words that my friend Turquoise Spectrum must speak. I do not know what he will say, except that he says they are urgent words." In the council chamber, Rockson said, "I turn the podium over to the distinguished representative of the Glowers."

The strange inside-out being came up to the podium as Rockson left. The Glower leader was *imposing*. People were uneasy and restive, curious perhaps, but not awed;

more afraid and confused.

Until he began speaking directly into each mind. That sobered them up plenty fast!

"PEOPLE OF CENTURY CITY, I SPEAK TO YOU ON A GRAVE MATTER OF CONCERN TO ALL. THE GREATEST ENEMY OF LIFE FORMS ON THIS PLANET, A MAN WHOM YOU ALL BELIEVE TO BE DEAD, IS NOT DEAD. I SPEAK OF KILLOV, MASTER OF DEATH. HE SURVIVED THE TIDAL WAVE UN-LEASHED BY YOUR BRAVE FIGHTERS AND IS GATHERING STRENGTH RIGHT NOW. SOON WILL COME A CHALLENGE TO THE VERY SURVIVAL OF THE ENTIRE WORLD. WE GLOWERS CANNOT HELP YOU MEET THIS CHALLENGE. IT IS NOT IN OUR CAPACITY, YET WE CAN WARN YOU. ONLY ONE BEING IS CAPABLE OF CHALLENGING THE FORCE OF DARKNESS AND THAT IS ROCKSON. DESTINY HAS CHOSEN HIM FOR THIS TASK. PRAY THAT HE IS UP TO IT. I HEAR MANY QUESTIONS IN YOUR MINDS. THERE IS NOT TIME FOR QUESTIONS. THIS IS ALL I HAVE TO SAY, ALL I CAN SAY ON THIS MATTER. NOW I SHALL LEAVE."

Thus ended the first address of an alien being to the council.

Just Rockson and Zydeco and Archer walked the Glower leader up the green-lit ramp to the western entrance to the city. As the doors opened to the twilit sky, Turquoise took off the shoulder pack he carried, full of supplies he had asked for at Century City, and set it down. He opened it up and lifted out a set of wire coat hangers and a box of aluminum foil. He held them forth to Rockson and said, "THIS IS MY GIFT TO YOU. TAKE IT. I CANNOT STATE THIS TOO STRONGLY," Turquoise added. "NEVER BE WITHOUT THESE NEARBY."

Rockson couldn't believe it. Why was the Glower handing him such mundane objects? Were they really what they seemed? But he graciously stepped forward and took the offered things. "Thank you," he said, rather perplexed, "but—"

"YOU WILL HAVE NEED OF THESE THINGS, ROCKSON. NEVER BE WITHOUT THEM," Turquoise repeated solemnly.

Rockson examined the objects. One hand held a few dozen wire coat hangers, the kind that come back from the dry-cleaners in B-section of Century City. The C.C. brand aluminum foil was just that — the kind you use to wrap leftovers in. "I don't understand . . . why should I need — ?"

"NEVER BE WITHOUT THEM," repeated the Turquoise Spectrum. "WHEN YOU NEED THEM, YOU WILL UNDERSTAND." He turned slightly and gauged the breeze coming in the open doorway. "THE WEATHER IS WARMING. I MUST LEAVE YOU NOW, FRIENDS. MY SHIP MUST REACH HOME BEFORE THE SNOWS ARE UTTERLY GONE, ELSE THE OTHER-DIMENSIONAL WORMS ARE A THREAT TO THE UNARMED SHIP. GOOD-BYE FRIENDS. GOOD LUCK, AS YOU SAY. BUT I SAY MUCH AS ALREADY BEEN DETERMINED, *SO MAY IT BEND YOUR WAY.*"

Rockson felt a tug in his heart. Of course they could never touch, but Rock almost wanted to run to the being and give him a big hug and squeeze. His inside-out, palpitating, blue-glowing friend had saved his life, taken him on such wonderful journeys, mental and spiritual. But that hug, sadly, could not be. So instead Rockson nodded and with great emotion shaking his words, simply said, "Good-bye."

Turquoise turned, strode into the entranceway winds, and stood there, and then he turned, silhouetted in the first glimmer of stars, and raised his right-hand palm so that it was facing them. Out of that upraised palm came a blue glow, a swirling spiral pattern. "GOOD-BYE AND ETERNAL FAREWELL, ROCKSON, ZYDECO, ARCHER . . . I WILL NEVER SEE YOU AGAIN ON THIS PLANE OF EXISTENCE."

The swirling pattern in his hand shot forth, then divided into three rays that shot outward from the palm toward each of the humans. When the ray hit Rockson, a gentle, soft pleasure spread in his mind like menthol hitting a sore throat. It faded slowly and when Rockson again brought his attention to the entranceway, Turquoise was *gone*.

The humans went outside and watched as Turquoise, already down the slope and across the half mile of snow between the mountain and his ice-crystal ship, climbed up the strange, pinkish rigging. Then they saw the triple sails being hauled into place and starting to catch the etheral winds. The flickering Milky Way's light seemed to catch and blossom in the sails. They watched in awe and sadness as silently the Glowers' ship sailed off into the swirling snow mists, heading northeast.

As the ship faded from sight in the vast loneliness, Rockson and his friends turned and walked back down the ramp toward the lights and sounds of Century City, Rockson carrying his bizarre gifts.

Rockson was especially quiet for the rest of the night, and retired to his room to stare at the ceiling.

I must save the world? I'm getting old, too old for this. I don't know if I can fight off Killov again. The man just won't die. He is the devil himself to have survived the tidal wave I unleashed on him in Africa!!

There was a gentle rapping on the door. Rockson pulled himself back from his thoughts, crushed out his cigarette. Would it be Rona or Kim?

He opened it up. It was *both* of them. They were wearing just the briefest of negligees. The tall, brassy redheaded goddess *and* the pert and lovely, petite, blue-eyed blond. He started to say something, but both females said, *"Shhhh."*

And then, giggling like schoolgirls, they pushed him gently back toward his bed.

ACTION ADVENTURE: WINGMAN #1-#6
by Mack Maloney

WINGMAN   (2015, $3.95)
From the radioactive ruins of a nuclear-devastated U.S. emerges a hero for the ages. A brilliant ace fighter pilot, he takes to the skies to help free his once-great homeland from the brutal heel of the evil Soviet warlords. He is the last hope of a ravaged land. He is Hawk Hunter . . . Wingman!

WINGMAN #2: THE CIRCLE WAR   (2120, $3.95)
A second explosive showdown with the Russian overlords and their armies of destruction is in the wind. Only the deadly aerial ace Hawk Hunter can rally the forces of freedom and strike one last blow for a forgotten dream called "America"!

WINGMAN #3: THE LUCIFER CRUSADE   (2232, $3.95)
Viktor, the depraved international terrorist who orchestrated the bloody war for America's West, has escaped. Ace pilot Hawk Hunter takes off for a deadly confrontation in the skies above the Middle East.

WINGMAN #4: THUNDER IN THE EAST   (2453, $3.95)
The evil New Order is raising a huge mercenary force to reclaim America, and Hawk Hunter, the battered nation's most fearless top gun fighter pilot, takes to the air to prevent this catastrophe from occurring.

WINGMAN #5: THE TWISTED CROSS   (2553, $3.95)
"The Twisted Cross," a power-hungry neo-Nazi organization, plans to destroy the Panama Canal with nuclear time bombs unless their war chests are filled with stolen Inca gold. The only route to saving the strategic waterway is from above—as Wingman takes to the air to rain death down upon the Cross' South American jungle stronghold.

WINGMAN #6: THE FINAL STORM   (2655, $3.95)
Deep in the frozen Siberian wastes, last-ditch elements of the Evil Empire plan to annihilate the Free World in one final rain of nuclear death. Trading his sleek F-16 fighter jet for a larger, heavier B-1B supersonic swing-wing bomber, Hawk Hunter undertakes his most perilous mission.

Available wherever paperbacks are sold, or order direct from the Publisher. Send cover price plus 50¢ per copy for mailing and handling to Zebra Books, Dept. 3074, 475 Park Avenue South, New York, N.Y. 10016. Residents of New York, New Jersey and Pennsylvania must include sales tax. DO NOT SEND CASH.